'You're quite ruthless, aren't you?'

'If that's the way you see it.' Reece sounded amused. 'I don't believe in holding back. Life's too short. And before you say it, I'm aware that's a cliché.'

'I wasn't going to say it,' she denied. 'I...wasn't going to say anything.'

'Not even no?' The amusement was still there. 'I'll take heart from that.'

TROUBLE ON TOUR

BY
KAY THORPE

MILLS & BOON LIMITED
ETON HOUSE   18-24 PARADISE ROAD
RICHMOND   SURREY   TW9 1SR

First published in Great Britain 1991
by Mills & Boon Limited

© Kay Thorpe 1991

Australian copyright 1991
Philippine copyright 1991
This edition 1991

ISBN 0 263 77032 X

Set in Times Roman 10 on 12 pt.
01-9103-54080 C

Made and printed in Great Britain

CHAPTER ONE

SEEN from the top of the steeply sloping street, the San Francisco bay area lay exposed in panoramic detail, with Alcatraz as its focal point and grim reminder of times past and gone.

It was remarkable how quickly the city had recovered from the earthquake a year ago, Lisa acknowledged, feeling her stomach give its familiar lurch as she headed the car across the flattened intersection to take the next plunging stretch. Remarkable too how untouched the taller, more modern buildings had been, built to flex with the movement rather than stand firm, from what she understood. Whatever, it had worked.

Knowing that the same thing could happen again at almost any time should be off-putting, she supposed, yet it made little difference to her desire to stay on. There was risk everywhere, of one kind or another. Not that wanting to stay was the be all and end all. To live and work in the States was a goal not easily achieved by an alien these days.

Jane had been lucky to manage a whole five years without being caught out by Immigration, and luckier still to be absolved under one of the periodic amnesties, and granted her green card. Lisa doubted her own ability to withstand the strain of illegality. If this temporary job came off it might at least be a step in the right direction. If nothing else, it would enable her to see rather more of the country than she might achieve under her own steam.

The traffic-lights ahead were flashing to amber. Not wholly into the habit of accelerating through before the red, Lisa wavered and lost her nerve, slamming on the brakes. Had she not been wearing a seatbelt, the jolt as the car behind rammed into her rear end would have catapulted her through the windscreen. As it was, she found her own vehicle pushed out across the intersection by the sheer force of the impact, to the tune of blaring horns as cars coming in the other direction were forced to stop.

Shock kept her motionless in her seat for what seemed like whole minutes but could only have been bare seconds, because even as she forced herself to open the car door and slide out, the driver of the car behind was only just getting out himself. Tall and dark-haired, the man moved forward to briefly examine the front end of his own vehicle before turning his attention to Lisa, who still stood nervelessly clutching the open door. His expression left little enough doubt of his thoughts; his tone simply serviced to underline them.

'I should know better than to rely on a woman's road sense!'

The sheer scathing force of the attack, and total lack of concern for her welfare, snapped Lisa out of any inclination towards blame-taking and into fighting mood herself. Green eyes flashing, she drew herself up to her full five feet six and let him have it right back, accents icily polite.

'You should know better, certainly, than to take it for granted that others are going to indulge in the same dangerous tactics you're so obviously accustomed to. The lights, in case you hadn't noticed, were at amber!'

'And you were going on through before you changed your mind at the last minute,' came the prompt and not unfounded reply. 'Did you never hear of checking behind you before slamming on the brakes—or isn't that a requirement where you come from?' He didn't wait for any answer, indicating his smashed front lights with a gesture that said it all. 'Hope you took out collision waiver insurance.'

'For one thing it isn't a hire car,' Lisa retorted. 'And, for another, I fail to see why I should be expected to foot the bill for your lack of anticipation.'

She was moving as she spoke, coming forward to check the state of her own vehicle and draw a breath of relief when she saw no immediate sign of damage. American car bumpers were made to ride in and out on impact, absorbing a lot of the shock. Had the man now facing her been driving one of his own country's models instead of the Italian sports job, he might now be in a similar position.

'Where I come from,' she tagged on coolly, 'rear-end shunts are always the fault of the one driving behind. Try claiming off your own insurance—always providing you have any.'

Steely grey eyes narrowed as he surveyed her finely sculpted features beneath the heavy fringe of red-brown hair. Lisa fought to stop the heat singeing her cheeks when he moved his gaze with deliberation down over the open neckline of her neat green and white shirtwaister to linger for an interminable second on the thrust of her breasts beneath the fine cotton. She knew what he was doing, and she knew why, but there was no way he was going to embarrass her into backing down from her stand. Judging from the cut of his lightweight suit, to say nothing of the car itself, he could afford the subsequent insurance loading far better than Jane could, anyway.

Steeling herself, she returned the scrutiny, assessing
the hard-boned masculinity of the lean features with a
faint fluttering sensation in the pit of her stomach. There
was no softness about the man at all. Over six feet in
height, with a broad-shouldered, lean-hipped build that
suggested latent power in the hidden muscle, he was too
much of everything. Mid-thirties, at a guess, but nearer
fifty in experience. The taunting flick of one thick dark
eyebrow as their eyes clashed and held was no help to
her equilibrium either.

The traffic brought to a halt by the accident was on
the move again, pulling around the out-thrust nose of
her car. About to suggest that she go and move it, Lisa
felt her heart sink like a stone as a motorcycle carrying
a uniformed officer came down the hill to pull in behind
the two stalled vehicles. A run-in with the law was the
last thing she needed.

Smart and cool in summer issue, the newcomer removed his helmet before strolling down to where the two
of them stood waiting. He was young, almost boyish in
appearance, short-cropped hair gleaming fair in the June
sunlight. He looked, Lisa reflected thankfully, anything
but officious.

'Having trouble, Mr Harland?' he asked, and sent her
heart plummeting anew. To be known by name to the
police could only mean one of two things, and she
doubted very much if her opponent was of the criminal
fraternity. A man of some importance, then, which was
hardly going to help her position.

'Nothing that can't be sorted with a little co-
operation,' came the smooth reply. 'We were just about
to exchange insurance details.'

'It isn't my car,' Lisa began, and could have bitten
her tongue as the officer gave her a searching scrutiny

before reaching into a breast pocket for notebook and pencil.

'Rented?' he asked succinctly.

She shook her head. 'It belongs to a friend.'

'Name and address?'

Green eyes met grey for a brief moment, and flickered away again. 'Mine, or hers?'

The officer allowed himself a faint grin. 'Both, I guess. Let's start with yours.'

Controlling the sigh, she said resignedly, 'Lisa Cunningham, of no fixed abode at present.'

This time the grin was missing. 'Is that a fact?'

'Only because I left my last address when I came out here on holiday,' she explained, already aware of having made a mistake in admitting that much. 'I'll be starting a new job in a different town when I go back home.' Which was no more than the truth, she reflected, *if* she had to go back.

'And the owner's name?'

'Jane Reynolds. Thirty-one hundred, Cecilia Street, Richmond.' She added swiftly, 'I'm staying with her.'

The young officer looked pensively at what he'd written. 'Guess I'd better see your driver's licence,' he said. 'And your passport too, if you're carrying it.'

She went back to fetch them from the handbag still resting on the front passenger seat. The two men were talking when she returned. Still minus the smile, the young officer took both documents from her, giving the licence a cursory glance before turning to the passport. Immigration had allowed her until the end of August, Lisa knew, so there was no cause for the tensing of muscle and sinew as the inserted departure slip was examined. She was here quite legally on extended holiday.

Nevertheless, she drew a shallow breath of relief when the documents were handed back with a crisp, 'Seems OK. Better tell the owner to bring the insurance papers down to the precinct.'

The older man made a sudden movement, as if grown tired of the whole situation. 'There's no physical injury,' he said. 'Supposing we just forget it? I'm going to be late for an appointment.'

The officer hesitated for a moment, then shrugged and closed his notebook. 'Guess it's OK with me, if that's what you want, Mr Harland.' To Lisa he added, 'Best get that car on its way, ma'am, before somebody piles into it.' Nodding to them both, he went back to his motorcycle.

Totally nonplussed, Lisa could summon neither word nor movement for a moment. It was left to her former opponent to say with irony, 'I'll take the gratitude as read.'

He was turning away before she found voice, any gratitude she might have felt swamped by righteous indignation at the assumption. 'Considering that the fault was yours to begin with, you're more than generous, *Mr* Harland!'

There was no reply. Lisa had the distinct impression that he didn't consider the sally worth the effort of even turning his head. Sliding behind the wheel of his own vehicle, he switched on the ignition and was next moment pulling out and round her to carry on over the intersection and out of sight down the hill before the lights could change against him.

Fuming, she got into the Chevrolet and backed up a little out of the traffic flow to await the next change. Were she honest with herself, the fault had been as much hers as his, but that was by the way. His whole attitude had been so typical of the male sex in relation to women drivers. She would have so loved to cut him down to size with a well-aimed riposte instead of the weak sarcasm that was all she had been able to come up with.

Forget him, advised common sense at that point. There was no point in getting het up over a situation over and done with. At the very least, Jane was off the hook for an expensive claim, although she would naturally have to tell her what had happened. That, however, could come later. For now, she was concerned only with the outcome of today's events.

Situated at Fisherman's Wharf, the travel agency for which Jane worked had its offices above the shop. Lisa was lucky enough to find a parking slot for the car within walking distance. The whole area was awash with tourists, the general atmosphere reminiscent of an English seaside resort in its promenade of shops and amusements and cheerful street vendors. If the job proved to be forthcoming, there were plenty of places at which to celebrate. If. Chances were they'd managed to come up with a replacement after all.

Jane signalled to her the moment she appeared in the office doorway. Leaving her desk, the other girl came over to draw Lisa aside with a look of controlled optimism on her pretty face.

'There's a real possibility,' she said. 'It all depends on whether management can swing it with the authorities. Our Mr Bucknell is desperate enough to try anything. Failing you, he might have to finish up taking over the tour himself! Anyway, he wants to see you right away.' She paused, tone altering a little. 'Incidentally, I told him you were already pretty well genned up on the actual route detail, so be prepared. You've done enough reading this last couple of days to bluff it through.'

'For which vote of confidence, thanks,' replied Lisa wryly. 'Where do I go?'

Her friend indicated the corridor on the other side of the glass partition. 'Last door along. Good luck!'

It wasn't luck she needed so much as an official willingness to bend the rules a little, thought Lisa, following directions. She wouldn't be taking a job away from a citizen because there was no one available capable of filling the position at such short notice. In any case, it was only going to be for a maximum of fifteen days. Her experience—plus a little bluff—had to have some bearing on the matter. Where else were they going to find a qualified courier at a loose end in mid-June?

Reaching the third and final door, she knocked, and was invited in. Mr Bucknell turned out to be a middle-aged man with a thinning hairline and a permanent frown etched between his brows. He invited her to a seat, leaning back in his chair to regard her with an expression she found discouraging.

'We managed to get permission for a temporary permit,' he acknowledged unexpectedly, 'but I'm still not sure we're doing the right thing.'

'Except that I'm the only choice left to you,' returned Lisa without particular inflection. 'I'm more than capable of taking the tour, Mr Bucknell. As Jane already told you, I've worked all over Europe.'

'Europe,' he said, 'not America.'

She smiled. 'People are people wherever they happen to be travelling. I understand there are several English parties due to take this particular tour too.'

He responded with a faint smile of his own. 'Some. Not that we segregate, although we do find it best if everyone sticks to the seat they're allocated throughout. Saves a lot of hassle. We run two smaller coaches per trip instead of the one large one so that we can take in less commercialised routes. Means there'll be a regular courier along too. We run two grades of tour, one luxury, one intermediate. This one is the "B" class.'

All of which she already knew via Jane, Lisa acknowledged, allowing herself to relax. She had the job, it was obvious. He really didn't have any other choice.

'You won't be sorry,' she promised. 'I'll give them the best time they ever had!'

'Good.' He added quickly, 'Providing you remember that the permit *is* only temporary, of course.'

'Of course,' she echoed, and mentally crossed her fingers. 'I'm just delighted to have the opportunity to see the country. Actually being paid for it is a bonus.'

'Good,' he said again. There was a momentary hesitation before he went on. 'I'm going to take Jane's word for it that you're conversant with the areas you'll be covering. Our clients don't expect a running commentary, but they will expect you to be able to tell them a few facts and figures. With regard to uniform, you'll have to take the closest fit from what we have available. There isn't going to be time for any alterations. The tour leaves the depot at nine o'clock sharp, Sunday morning. You'll need to be there by seven-thirty.'

There was more in the same vein, but Lisa listened with only half an ear. She was on her way. Two whole weeks on the road. Whatever happened afterwards, she would have that to look back on.

It was gone five-thirty when she finally left the office. Jane had waited for her. One look at Lisa's face was all she needed to tell her the news.

'Dinner is on me,' she said happily. 'It's likely to be the last leisurely meal you're going to get for a couple of weeks. You'll be too busy preparing tomorrow to think about eating. Let's go across to Pier 39. That Swiss place is quite good.'

The crowds outside had thickened if anything. This was the height of the tourist season, the wharf itself a must for all visitors to San Francisco. Fishing boat masts bobbed along the sea wall.

The air had cooled considerably from its daytime high. Evenings down here by the sea-front were apt to call for a wrap of some kind about the shoulders. July and August would bring the spectacular bay fogs curling up through the Golden Gate as the differing air temperatures clashed. Lisa wondered if she would still be here come the autumn.

Just a couple of blocks along the wharf, the boarded walks and festive market-place atmosphere of Pier 39 beckoned young and old alike. At this hour there was no great problem in securing a table in one of the restaurants overlooking the bay. Seated, with drinks in front of them, Jane raised her glass with a smile.

'Here's to good fortune. May it long continue!'

Lisa laughed, and lifted her own glass. 'I'll drink to that.' Putting it down again, she gave vent to a sigh of pure satisfaction. 'It's rotten to be making hay out of someone else's misfortune, but it isn't as if I'm stealing the job out from under her nose. She'll probably be over the virus by the time I get back.'

'And if she isn't, you'll simply have to fill in for her again on the next tour,' put in Jane, voicing the thought Lisa hadn't been about to put into words herself. 'Cross each bridge as you come to it. That's what I did. Who knows, they might decide you're so good at the job you're worth going out on a limb for.'

'And pigs might fly.' Lisa had no intention of betting on such long odds. 'If I don't get to stay on here, I might try Australia.'

Jane regarded her with sympathetic eyes. 'I don't blame you for wanting to make a break. This last year must have been hell for you.'

Lisa made a small, wry gesture and turned her gaze on the view up the bay to the vast arched span of Golden Gate Bridge. Since losing both parents in that car crash fourteen months ago, she had run a whole gamut of emotions. She wasn't over it, nor ever would be, but she was learning to live with it. This urge to start over somewhere new was a part of that readjustment. America had appealed for several reasons, of which Jane was by no means the least. Having a friend in a strange place was always a good thing.

The two of them had known each other since childhood. In some respects, they were as close as sisters might have been. A year older than her own twenty-four, Jane had thoroughly upset her own parents by her decision to try her luck in the States, although they had come round to it since. The invitation to spend the summer months in San Francisco had come at a time when Lisa herself was desperately in need of a change. She'd handed in her notice to the travel company for which she'd worked these last three years, and taken the plunge. Money wasn't an immediate problem. She had inherited a fair amount from the sale of the family home. All the same, she couldn't live off capital forever.

'I'm going to forget the whole thing for the next two weeks,' she said with resolve, bringing her attention back to the face across the table again, 'and just enjoy the experience. It's the only way I'm ever likely to get to see the sights I'm going to be seeing without going alone.'

She ticked off the places on her fingers. 'Lake Tahoe, Vegas, Grand Canyon, Los Angeles—to name but a few!'

'Sounds great,' Jane agreed. 'I half wish I was coming with you.'

Lisa laughed. 'I'll be back before you know it.'

All *too* soon, in fact, came the reflection, but that was something she would face when it happened.

The coach depot was off Leavenworth. Dropped outside the reception office by Jane promptly on the half-hour, Lisa took a long, slow breath before going on in. The uniform of pale beige and white cotton skirt and blouse felt cool and light, her low-heeled sandals comfortable. Tucked away in her suitcase were three more outfits, including a smart striped blazer for possible cooler occasions. She was allowed to wear her own clothes in the evenings, and at leisure, whenever that might be. With two nights in Las Vegas, for instance, there was going to be time to do her own thing.

The young man checking a file at the desk looked round at her entry, his good-looking face breaking into a smile as he took in her appearance. He was wearing the same beige and white cotton in the shape of slacks and shirt, his body lean and fit beneath. Thick blond hair, bleached even lighter at the front by the sun, enhanced his depth of tan.

'I guess you have to be Lisa Cunningham,' he said. 'Nice to have you aboard!'

Lisa smiled back at him gratefully. 'Nice to be given the chance. I'm only sorry it had to be under these circumstances. Have you heard how your usual partner is doing?'

'OK. She should be back on her feet in a few days.' He was studying her frankly as he spoke, blue eyes speculative. 'You've done this job back in England, they said.'

'I was employed by a British company,' she acknowledged, 'but I've worked all over Europe.'

'Something I wouldn't mind having a go at myself. I'm Dean Price, by the way. Single, solvent, and at your service, ma'am!' His grin was appealing, as well he knew. 'Put your case down, and we'll go over the passenger list together. Get to know a few names. It always helps, don't you find?'

'Every time,' Lisa agreed. She dropped her suitcase down by the side of the desk. 'What time are they likely to start arriving?'

'Any time after eight-thirty—with one or two sure to roll up late.' The shrug reflected little concern. 'With only a couple of hundred miles to go to Tahoe today, there's no great hassle. Have a seat. I'll fetch us some coffee.'

The coffee provided, fresh and excellent, albeit in plastic cups, two copies of the passenger list were produced and the check commenced. Most were couples, Lisa noted, with just a sprinkling of single names. Going through in alphabetical order as placed, she was halfway down the page before the name Harland came up and hit her in the face.

Coincidence, of course, she reassured herself. The man she had met two days ago had hardly been the type to be taking a tour such as this one. Just thinking about him made her bristle all over again.

Forget it, Jane had advised on being told the tale. There was no damage to her car, so no big deal. Men like that weren't worth a fig in her estimation. Lisa agreed with her, but the incident refused to be banished completely from her mind. She could still see his face: that sardonic tilt at the corners of the strong mouth. Not a man she ever wanted to meet up with again, and that was a fact!

There was plenty to occupy her mind over the following half-hour or so. The two drivers proved to be steady types, both in their mid-forties with years of experience in this line under their respective belts. With the coaches themselves, Lisa could find no fault. Each seating a maximum of twenty-four people, they boasted an on-board toilet in addition to a coffee-maker and soft drinks bar. The upholstery was spotless, the chrome-work gleaming, the whole impression one of comfort and caring. Compared with some of the transport she had been accustomed to using in Europe, these were luxury incorporated, she conceded. The 'A'-class tour must be *really* something!

'Same transport, just more up-market hotels,' Dean supplied when she asked. 'Considering the price differential, ours is the better value.' He gave her a slow smile, added meaningfully, 'I'd say I'm going to enjoy this trip more than most.'

Lisa returned the smile and ignored the undertone. Dean no doubt had most females eating out of his hand, but if he imagined for a moment that the two of them were about to become anything other than workmates, he could think again. She wanted no involvement of that nature.

Passengers began arriving. Lisa was impressed to note the organised manner in which their bags were taken from them immediately and stowed, leaving them free of encumbrance to drink coffee in the reception area and start getting to know one another. Friendships would be struck over the coming two weeks, maybe one or two even cemented. Americans were a gregarious race all round.

The British contingent, she knew, had spent the first three days of their holiday in San Francisco itself. Transportation from the hotel was included in the package. Five couples, and one family of four. Lisa was relieved to find that both junior members of the latter were in their teens. A tour of this nature was no place for small children—the travelling was too restrictive.

So far, the name of Harland had not been ticked of, she noted, glancing down the list. There were three people still to come, all of them singles, one of them a woman—the only lone woman on the tour. Name of Bellman, and a Miss. Lisa smiled to herself at the thought that crossed her mind. Matchmaking was not part of her duties. Nice if it happened though. It wouldn't be the first time.

The three arrived almost together around five minutes to the hour. First an elderly man who looked fit as a fiddle, next a beautifully made-up and coiffured blonde in a white linen suit scheduled to crease like mad within the first hour of sitting. Late twenties, Lisa judged fleetingly, and very sure of herself, then her attention shifted to the man who had followed her through the door, and she felt her heart give a sickening jerk.

The type to take this kind of trip or not, he was here. Why, she couldn't begin to imagine, because he looked anything but thrilled at the prospect. Not that his apparent lack of enthusiasm could in any way match hers, came the wry thought. The gilt had just been rubbed off the gingerbread.

The taut-skinned features acquired a new and unreadable expression as their eyes met across the room. He said something to the woman in front of him, then came on over to where Lisa was standing, clipboard in her hand.

'Sandra Bellman, Reece Harland,' he announced succinctly. 'How come they're allowing a British courier to take the tour out?'

'English,' Lisa corrected with a cool composure she was far from feeling inside. 'I'm filling in on a temporary basis for the regular courier who was taken ill. All legal and above board, Mr Harland. If you'd like to take a seat for a few minutes, we'll be boarding shortly.'

He gave her a level appraisal. 'You've done this job before?'

'Of course. I'd hardly be here now if I hadn't.' She was doing her best to hang on to her poise. 'You'll none of you be losing out, I can promise you.'

The slow, slanting smile was a spur to the antagonism already boiling inside her. 'I guess we should be grateful you're not driving.'

Lisa drew in a deep and steadying breath as he moved back to take a seat beside the Bellman woman. He was on her coach too, which wasn't going to help. She caught Dean looking at her a little oddly, and made an effort to relax her expression. Awkward customers were nothing new. The fact that this particular one set her teeth on edge more than most was neither here nor there. She could deal with it.

Seat allocations had been made at source. Lisa was unsurprised to see Reece Harland sharing with the blonde and beautiful Miss Bellman. The two of them obviously knew each other, yet the bookings had been made separately according to the sheet. Separate rooms, for sure; it was right down here in black and white.

Not her business, anyway, she told herself firmly. So far as she was concerned, Reece Harland existed only as a passenger. He would be treated with courtesy and consideration because that was her job, but there would be none of the friendly familiarity she was accustomed to developing with people over the course of a two-week tour. In fact, the less she had to do with him, the better.

CHAPTER TWO

THEY got under way at nine-fifteen. Nice going, as Dean declared before climbing aboard his own home from home for the next fifteen days.

Busy with the coffee-machine at the rear of the coach, Lisa could only steal an occasional glimpse out of the side window as they rolled smoothly along North Point down to the Embarcadero and turned towards the Oakland Bridge. Traffic was light on this bright and sunny weekend morning, although the same could not be said of the pavements. This part of town took the brunt of the tourist trade.

The coffee was made by the time they reached the bridge. It was just as spectacular as Golden Gate in Lisa's estimation.

She served drinks and biscuits once they were over and heading up the inner coastline. Allowing for lunch at Rancho Cordova, they should make Tahoe no later than four. Two nights' stopover gave a whole day free in between for everyone to please themselves, although a boat trip on the lake was scheduled for those who fancied it. Altogether a satisfactory arrangement. Lake Tahoe was reputedly one of the most beautifully situated expanses of inland water in the world.

Reece Harland asked for coffee, as did the woman occupying the window seat at his side. The pair of them stood out like sore thumbs amid this crowd, Lisa reflected as she poured the hot liquid. Already the four couples at the rear were chatting like old friends.

By the time they left Tahoe, the whole coachload would probably have relaxed into the same easygoing mood. Apart from these two that was. She had a feeling they would stay well clear of any kind of party spirit.

Grey eyes lifted to hers as she handed over the cups. Lisa schooled herself not to react to the derisive glint.

'Cookie?' she asked with deliberation, proffering the box. 'There's chocolate chip, or plain shortbread.'

'Hardly an inspired choice,' drawled the blonde-haired Bellman women. 'Yours—or the company's?'

Lisa forced a smile, a light rejoinder. 'We'll be making a brief stop in an hour or so, if you fancy something a little more appetising, Miss Bellman.'

The other shrugged. 'I don't eat between meals.'

'You don't eat all that much at them,' came the dry comment from the man at her side, eliciting a laugh and a total alteration in attitude as she turned her head to look at him.

'I have to watch my figure, honey!'

'Along with the rest of us.' The tone was bland, expression equally so. 'I'm not complaining.' His glance came back to Lisa, who was still standing there with the box of biscuits. 'Not for me either, thanks.'

Watching your weight too? it was on the tip of her tongue to remark, but she bit it back. Not only would it be unprofessional to indulge in that kind of repartee, but unmerited to boot. The light-coloured, beautifully tailored trousers and matching shirt he was wearing emphasised the taut muscularity of a body any man could be justifiably proud of. That it failed to impress her was quite by the way.

Barry Goddard, the driver, gave her a thumbs-up through the mirror as she completed her first round and came to take her seat at the front for a while.

'You're doing fine, kid,' he said over a shoulder. 'Just fine!'

So far, so good, Lisa accepted. There was a long way to go yet.

The morning went smoothly enough. Luncheon was taken in a roadside hotel on the outskirts of the little township. Dean had already secured a table for the two of them, Lisa found on entering the pleasant restaurant with its cool green and white décor and country cottage ambience. She chose a sliced beef salad from the extensive menu, and tried not to notice that Reece Harland and his lady-love were seated at the next table.

In point of fact, the relationship between the two wasn't anywhere near that cut and dried, she was bound to acknowledge. They were travelling together, yet separately too. Sandra Bellman's reservation had been made the day after his, according to the files, both of them during the last week. A married woman stealing an illicit vacation with her lover, maybe? That might explain the necessity of keeping the bookings separate.

'You haven't heard a word I've said, have you?' accused Dean, jerking her out of her thoughts and back to present company. He looked faintly aggrieved, obviously unaccustomed to such a state of affairs. 'Are you always this quiet?'

Lisa smiled and shook her head. 'Sorry, I was miles away. What were you saying?'

'I asked if you knew about the company take-over,' he repeated, slightly mollified by the attention she was giving him now.

Green eyes widened a little. 'No, I didn't. Jane never mentioned it either.'

'Probably because she isn't in the know. I only picked up on it myself by accident. One of the big combines.

According to my source, the deal's already been clinched. We might even get back to find ourselves out of a job. They'll have their own staff ready to take over.'

Considering her temporary status, she had nothing to lose herself, Lisa conceded, but Jane was another matter. Jobs weren't so plentiful that she could simply walk straight into another.

'Is that the usual procedure over here?' she asked.

Dean shrugged. 'It's been known. There'll be changes made, for sure. You can bet somebody's going to suffer. These conglomerates are run by the buck—and I don't mean the written variety!'

He could be wrong, Lisa told herself. He had to be wrong. Take-over or not, no company was going to turn round and sack staff wholesale. All the same, the secrecy gave rise to some concern. These things were normally the subject of speculation by the media for weeks before the actual deal was done.

'This tuna is off!' exclaimed Sandra Bellman in unnecessarily carrying tones. 'Not surprising in a place like this, I suppose. You'd think they'd at least choose a decent venue!'

Lisa got to her feet with some reluctance. Dealing with such matters was part of her job, and normally accepted as such, but why did it have to happen to Miss Bellman, of all people?

Reece Harland hadn't said a word. His expression, as green eyes briefly clashed with grey, was neutral. Lisa had the feeling he was deliberately waiting to see how she would handle the affair.

The fish both looked and smelled fresh enough. Picking up a clean fork from the nearest empty table, Lisa looked Sandra Bellman in the eye. 'Do you mind if I try a piece?

'I tell you it's off!' declared the other. 'That should be enough.'

They were attracting attention both from the staff and other diners. Lisa seized the path of least resistance, and went to speak to the waitress.

'One of our passengers finds her fish a little strong,' she said quietly. 'Perhaps you could bring her something else.'

'Sure,' agreed the girl, not in the least put out. 'I'll get the menu back.'

Sandra looked somewhat less than delighted to have the offending dish removed without further fuss. She'd settle for coffee, she declared when asked to make a second choice. After the fish, she didn't feel like eating anything else.

'Everything all right with you, Mr Harland?' queried Lisa drily of the man still sitting there without a word. 'I see you chose the beef salad. Mine is very good.'

It was obvious from the sudden glint in his eyes that the intonation wasn't lost on him. 'It's fine,' he agreed. 'There isn't a lot can go wrong with beef. What time do you reckon on landing at Tahoe?'

'Around four, as in the itinerary.' She couldn't resist adding the last. If people bothered to read the literature supplied they wouldn't need to ask superfluous questions.

With the dark head at a lower level, she could see the slight wave in the thickness of his hair. There was no sign of dressing, just crisp cleanliness. Nice to run one's fingers through, came the irrelevant thought, as swiftly discarded. He held no attraction for her; none at all!

One of the other passengers called her over to ask the same question he had just asked. By the time she got back to her seat, Dean had finished his main course and was on to dessert.

'Don't let them roust you,' he advised as she picked up her knife and fork again to tackle the huge portion of thinly sliced pink and juicy meat. 'We're not here to nursemaid.'

He was wrong about that too, Lisa reflected with wry humour. This job called for all the qualities essential to the caring profession.

The hotel boasted a small gift shop. Persuading some people out of there and back on to the coaches at the appropriate hour was a task in itself. Dean was little help. They'd come, he said, when they were good and ready, not before. Folks disliked being hassled.

Like it or not, Lisa was determined they should stick to schedule as closely as possible. The drivers were governed by official regulations regarding hours on the road. They didn't want to be kept hanging around any longer than need be.

Ushering the last lingerer out into the sunshine, with due admiration given to purchases, she saw that both Reece Harland and Sandra Bellman had got back off the bus and were sitting on a bench set under one of the trees shading the hotel frontage.

'Thought me may as well take advantage of the fresh air while we waited,' said the former easily, getting to his feet. 'It's doubtful we'll reach Tahoe by four now, but who's counting?'

'I am,' returned Lisa crisply. 'Would you like to get back on board, please?'

His smile was infuriating. 'Sure.' He saw his blonde companion on first, standing back to indicate that Lisa should follow her. 'After you.'

He came up behind her as she mounted the two steps—too close for comfort. Catching her heel on the metal trim, she stumbled and would have fallen if an arm hadn't snaked about her waist from the rear, yanking her up against the hard male body and holding her there for an interminable second before releasing her.

'Watch your step,' said a sardonic voice in her ear. 'We don't want another accident.'

Not deigning to reply, Lisa made room for him to pass her, watching his retreating back up the aisle with a weakness in her lower limbs that had nothing to do with the near fall. In that brief moment of contact she had been conscious of him the way she had never been conscious of any man before: like an electric shock, was the nearest she could come to the sensation aroused in her. She could still feel the pressure of his arm at her waist.

Pure chemical reaction, she told herself. Nothing more. He probably hadn't felt a thing himself—a thought giving rise to an emotion she didn't want to examine too closely.

The landscape became even more rugged as the altitude increased. Even now, in mid-June, the mountains retained their snow caps, brilliant white in the sunlight. Every bend revealed a new vista.

Lisa's heart was in her throat more than once as the road skirted drops of several hundred feet, with only a low metal rail as a barrier. That the driver was well-accustomed to the route, and therefore unlikely to be affected by the same vertigo, was at least some comfort.

Topping the pass at seven thousand feet, they had their first glimpse of Lake Tahoe in the middle distance, a vast expanse of brilliant blue ringed with mountains that seemed to touch the sky. A skier's paradise up until early May, Lisa had read. Even later some years. Difficult to equate the heat out there now with the images of winter. Even more difficult still to consider that in a few days' time they would be experiencing temperatures of up to a hundred and twenty-five degrees in some places, and still be in California.

A pull-in had been constructed where the road began its main descent. Big enough to take both coaches, together with the several private cars already parked, it was marked on Lisa's itinerary as a ten-minute stop for photographs.

Glad of the opportunity to stretch her legs, she walked down to the far end of the area away from the group jostling for position along the perimeter wall, to set up her own shot of the stupendous view. Not that a compact camera was going to do it justice, she knew, but the snap would at least remind her.

At this height the sun's heat was diffused enough to make it enjoyable. Lisa leant against a rock to gaze her fill of the scene. She was unaware of anyone approaching until the newcomer spoke.

'Finding it too much for you?'

She had stiffened on the first syllable, but she made no immediate move. 'If you mean the view,' she said evenly, 'I imagine everyone does the first time.'

'I meant the job,' Reece Harland returned. 'I was under the impression it entailed keeping an eye on your clients.'

Straightening, she turned to look at the man, resenting his attitude even while recognising a certain validity in what he was saying. 'You're all adults, Mr Harland. I doubt very much if anyone is going to come to any harm in ten minutes.'

He had halted a few feet away, stance easy, expression anything but. 'Hardly the point. We're paying for a *con-*

ducted tour. In my book, that means being available, not skulking off alone every opportunity.'

'I've never *skulked* anywhere in my life!' she exclaimed furiously, then caught herself up in realisation of her position. She had never allowed herself to be provoked into speaking to a client like that before either. Swallowing her ire, she added with control, 'You're quite right, of course. I should be back there ministering to your needs. Was there anything special you wanted, Mr Harland?'

A spark leapt in the grey eyes. 'I was speaking collectively not personally,' he said, 'but since you ask—'

'Reece!' Sandra Bellman was way back up by the coaches, but her cry carried loud and clear. 'We're ready to go.'

Whatever he had been about to say was discarded in favour of a shrug and cool, 'Your cue, I think.'

They walked back to the coaches together, the air between them simmering with Lisa's barely concealed animosity. The man was an autocrat, out and out. Full value for money, he was demanding, full value he should have, whatever it took. From now on she would make darn sure he had no further cause for complaint!

Sandra watched them coming with an all too easily recognisable expression on her face. Naked jealousy was distasteful in anyone, Lisa thought—especially when it had no foundation. She switched on a smile with which to face the people filtering back on to the coach, leaving the two of them to sort out their own differences. The woman was more than welcome to him!

Despite the relative closeness of the lake as seen from above, it took a further hour to reach it. South Lake Tahoe was a resort in itself, with hotels and motels, shops and restaurants stretched along the shoreline. No more than a couple of miles north lay the Nevada state line and casino area.

No doubt many would be eager to try their luck, reflected Lisa as they turned into the car park of the hotel selected by the tour operators. The possibility, remote though it might be, of winning one of the huge jackpots publicised by the media was a great temptation. For herself, she was content to wait until Vegas, although even then she would be investing no more than twenty dollars or so. Losing a fortune on the chance of making another was a mug's game.

One of a large American chain, and in a low to medium price bracket, the hotel itself was clean and comfortable and well-equipped. The rooms allocated to the tour hosts each contained two queen-sized beds; they also, Lisa noted, had communicating doors.

She opened up her side with resignation when Dean knocked on it at six o'clock. Like herself, he had changed from uniform into his own clothing. The spotless white trousers and black shirt left partially open on a glimpse of golden brown chest were so synonymous with her expectations, she had to conceal a smile. He had missed his true vocation, if she didn't miss a guess. Role-playing was second nature to him.

'How about the two of us running up to the state line for dinner and a little flutter?' he asked.

'In these?' Lisa asked guilelessly, indicating her high heels. 'I don't think they'd stand up to it.'

'Sharp as they come!' He was laughing, but obviously not all that much amused. 'You know what I mean. The night is ours.'

Lisa knew exactly what he meant. Whether he was in the habit of enjoying a closer relationship with his usual

partner was none of her business, but he wasn't about
to make time with her.

'One of us should perhaps stay around base in case
anyone needs anything,' she said a little lamely. 'I don't
mind taking it on this evening, if you feel like visiting
a casino or two.'

His shrug was philosophical. 'You're going to find it
a waste of time, but suit yourself. See you in the
morning.'

He wouldn't, Lisa thought as she closed the door
again, be spending the whole evening alone. Not looking
the way he did. Strange that she felt absolutely no pull
towards him at all. She was probably one of a very few.

Apart from a touch of lipstick, she was ready to go
herself. She checked her appearance in the mirror before
departing the room, smoothing the skirt of her white
linen dress over slim hips. The tan already acquired over
the past couple of weeks lent her skin a healthy glow
and made her eyes look an even deeper green than
normal.

Smooth and glossy, her hair hugged the shape of her
head in a bob that was very nearly a shingle. Easy to
manage, the stylist has said, which it was. All she had
to do was comb it after washing to have it back in perfect
shape. Better by far, she had to admit, than the longer
style she had had for years, but it was taking a little
getting used to all the same. It even made her appear
taller than her customary five and a half feet.

She found the hotel restaurant already almost full
when she got there. The English family were seated at
a table set for six. Mrs Fuller beckoned her over, indicating the spare settings.

'We didn't order yet,' she said with a friendly warmth.
'Why don't you join us?'

'Yes, do,' echoed her husband. A large, confident-looking man in his early forties, he gave vent to a chuckle as his eyes sought those of his son seated opposite. 'We'd all be delighted, wouldn't we, Ben?'

The boy flushed crimson and made no reply. He was about fourteen years old, Lisa judged, and more like his mother in looks and colouring than his father. She took the seat with a word of thanks, careful not to look at Ben directly while the blush still suffused his face.

His sister made no such effort. Old enough, at sixteen or so, to know better, she added fuel to the fire by saying glibly, 'You've gone all hot, Ben. Shall I ask them to turn up the air-conditioning?'

'We weren't expecting to find an English courier on the tour,' put in Mrs Fuller without haste. 'How long have you been over here?'

By the time Lisa had explained her position, and the waitress had taken their order, Ben was back to normal colour and beginning to relax. Fourteen was an awkward age, thought Lisa with sympathy, recalling her own emotional traumas. She'd once developed an instant crush on a student teacher, and been prone to the same embarrassing rush of blood whenever eye-to-eye contact had been established. Family teasing, as in the case of father and sister, was the last thing needed.

She excused herself on the grounds of having paper-work to complete as soon as the meal was over, and returned to her room to comply with that very need. Dean would no doubt have his own routine; it certainly wasn't up to her to worry about when and how he was going to fit in the mandatory daily report. He was probably right, though, about the waste of time in hanging around the hotel all evening. Any information needed regarding the area could be gleaned from the front desk far more easily. Regardless of what Reece Harland might think, they were entitled to some off-duty time considering they were on call all day and every day.

Neither he nor his travelling companion had been in evidence in the restaurant. Not that it concerned her. After this afternoon's episode, she wanted as little to do with the pair of them as possible. Their reasons for taking this trip were still obscure. Of the two, Sandra Bellman seemed to be making most of the running. A woman rather too possessive to hold a man like that for long, in Lisa's view. You didn't put curbs on a bull elephant!

She spent an hour or two exploring the area within walking distance of the hotel, returning around ten when the shops in the nearby square began to close down for the night. Any fatigue she might have felt had passed by the time she was ready for bed. Lying there listening to the breeze rustling the tree leaves outside her window, she knew she wasn't going to sleep. There was an inexplicable restlessness inside her.

Her watch said midnight when she finally gave in and got up again to don trousers and light sweater against the night air. A stroll down to the beach she hadn't yet seen might do the trick. At the very least it would occupy her mind.

The lobby lights themselves had been dimmed, the desk left unmanned, although she could hear voices coming from somewhere. A rear door gave access to the pool area. Beyond the patio, a fence gate bore the sign: 'To the beach'. Following the well-trodden path through the trees, Lisa sniffed pleasurably at the pine-scented air. The lake was six thousand feet above sea level, and the night temperature was cool but not chilly. Stimulating was the word.

Reaching the wide stretch of yellow sand stretching for some half-mile around the curve of the shoreline, she paused for a moment or two to view the moonlit scene. The opposite side of the lake was a jagged black line in the far distance, with twelve miles of silvered water between. Only Titicaca in Bolivia lay at a higher level than this inland sea.

A sudden movement a few yards away on her left made her heart jerk because she had thought herself alone. The moon choosing that same moment to disappear behind a passing cloud didn't help. A shape detached itself from the side of a tree, and resolved into human form. Recognition was more a matter of instinct than visual affirmation.

'Sleepwalking, or just taking an early morning stroll?' asked the familiar sardonic voice.

Recovery was swift. 'Wasn't it you yourself,' she returned smoothly, 'who demanded constant attention? I'm just doing my job, Mr Harland, and making sure you don't come to any harm out here in the dark.'

There was a hint of amusement in the easy answer. 'That British backchat of yours is going to land you in trouble one of these days.'

'English,' she corrected without altering her tone. 'Try to get it right for once. British covers the Scots and Welsh too.'

'I stand corrected.' He mimicked her accent, the words clipped and precise, dropping back into his native inflection to add softly, 'You're treading a very narrow path.'

'Meaning I'm in danger of being reported for not showing the deference you consider right and proper?' She shook her head, suddenly and recklessly uncaring of future chances. 'I'm purely temporary, Mr Harland.

I don't have to kowtow to anyone in order to preserve my job. Just for the record, I fancied a stroll because I couldn't sleep, not because I saw you heading this way in the moonlight. If I'd known you were here, I'd have taken another direction.'

The silence which followed that little outburst was brief but weighted. He just stood there looking at her, features obscured by the darkness. When he did speak it was with deceptive mildness.

'Are you always this prickly, or is there something about me that particularly bugs you?'

Aware of the increased rate of her pulses, she made an effort to collect herself. 'If anything about you does bug me, as you so succinctly put it, it's your assumption that all women are fools,' she retorted. 'I'm not interested in your reasons for taking this tour, but——'

'Why not the usual reason?' he cut in. 'The scenery is surely worth seeing.'

'If you haven't already, and wanted to, you'd be doing your own driving,' she said with more certainty than grammatical clarity. 'You're as far removed from the regular, run-of-the-mill tourist as they come. I don't need a degree in psychology to see that. Neither,' she added imprudently, 'is Miss Bellman any sightseer. In fact, I'd go so far as to say it bores her into the ground.'

'I thought you said you weren't interested?' The tone was mocking now. 'Seems you've been giving the two of us a whole lot of thought.'

Lisa bit her lip. She had laid herself wide open to that. 'Considering you both of you obviously have something to hide, it's hardly surprising,' she came back, casting discretion to the winds. 'There must be better ways of getting away together than this.'

Coming out from behind the cloud, the moon highlighted an ominous spark in the grey eyes. 'It's no part
of your job to make rash assumptions. Whatever the
relationship between Miss Bellman and me, it's strictly
our affair.'

Her smile was pure honey. 'You said it. *I'll* say goodnight, Mr Harland. I think I should sleep now.'

The sand deadened his footsteps, but he must have
moved like lightning because he was on her before she
completed the about-face. The hand seizing her upper
arm was steel-like in its grip, dragging her round again.
Her other arm was taken in a similar grip, and she felt
herself lifted on her toes to meet the strong hard mouth
coming down on hers in a punishing kiss.

How long it lasted, she wasn't entirely sure. Her whole
attention was concentrated on the sensations racing
through her. His chest was squashing her breasts, his
thigh muscles like iron against the quivering weakness
of her own. There was nothing even remotely lover-like
in the embrace, yet she found a deep down part of her
responding to the sheer force of him.

Her voice felt locked in her throat when he finally let
her go. She couldn't even raise a sound of protest.
Shaken, she could only gaze at him, eyes wide and dark
in a face turned alabaster by the moonlight.

'That,' he said softly, 'is what happens to little girls
who get above themselves. You'd like lesson two even
less, so just put a curb on that tongue of yours from
now on. I'm a paying customer. That entitles me to a
certain deference, even if this job isn't all that important
to you.'

The suspicion that he might have a valid point was no
aid to her at the moment. Her mouth was on fire, her

whole equilibrium shot to pieces. Still speechless, she turned on her heel to go, making a bare four paces before tripping over a hidden tree root and measuring her length with a thud that drove what breath she had managed to regain right out of her again. She was almost in tears from sheer humiliation when he lifted her back to her feet.

'Just get your hands off me, and keep them off!' she shot at him. 'Touch me again, and I'll bring a charge of sexual harassment against you!'

'You'd never make it stick,' he said, complying with the demand. '*You* followed *me* out here, remember?'

'That's not true,' declared Lisa with heat, 'and you know it!'

'No, I don't know it.' He was totally in control of the situation, and enjoying it. 'For my book, you provoked me into going for you because you're a frustrated young woman badly in need of a man. Given other circumstances, I might have been more forthcoming, but I guess it could become complicated, considering.'

There was little point, Lisa conceded there and then, in continuing to deny the imputation. Whether he really believed it himself or was simply taunting her was immaterial. What mattered was retrieving her dignity—or what was left of it.

'I doubt if frustration would draw me to a man like you under any circumstances, Mr Harland,' she stated with delicate emphasis. 'Irresistible though you may be to your own countrywomen, we English appreciate finesse. Goodnight again.'

This time she managed to walk away without falling over anything. He made no attempt to follow her, which fact left her oddly deflated. Her lips felt slightly swollen, the soft tissue bruised. She could only hope there would be no visible reminder by morning. Facing him again was going to be difficult enough without that.

CHAPTER THREE

DESPITE not sleeping until the early hours, and even then only fitfully, Lisa was down for breakfast before eight.

The lake cruise was scheduled to depart at ten-thirty. Before that, she had to marshal her party, few of whom were in evidence at present. She was relieved to find both Reece Harland and his companion absent from the restaurant. Whether they would be taking the cruise, she had no idea. It was included in the overall tour price, but that didn't make it mandatory. Some people still preferred to spend the free days doing things their own way. Hopefully, those two would be of that ilk.

Dean put in an appearance some fifteen minutes later. He looked, Lisa thought, as fresh as the proverbial daisy.

'Have a good evening?' she asked casually when he came to join her at the table.

'Profitable,' he acknowledged. 'You should have been there. My luck was definitely in.' He paused, eyeing her with a certain calculation. 'Would you do me a favour?'

'If I can,' she said.

'You can. Question is, will you take over both parties for the cruise this morning? All you have to do is make sure as many get off at the end as got on. The commentary's given by a crew member.'

Lisa shrugged. 'I don't suppose it really needs two of us to keep an eye on them.'

'Thanks.' The blue eyes were lit by satisfaction. 'I met this girl last night. She——'

'Say no more!' Lisa held up a hand in mock prohibition. 'My ears are too tender.'

'Like little pink shells,' he agreed. 'Just made for kissing.' It was his turn to hold up a hand, shaking his head in a parody of wistful regret. 'No go area, right?'

'Right.' She added lightly, 'And having established that much, perhaps we can just be good friends?'

The agreement was equally light. 'Why not? There has to be a first time for everything.'

About to make some quip in return, Lisa felt her face go suddenly warm as she caught sight of the man just entering the restaurant. Wearing white shorts and T-shirt, he looked no less a man of command. His legs were long and strong and bronzed, the muscles of his thighs clearly defined as he walked across to a table in the wake of the hostess. Remembering the feel of them last night made her skin tingle even now.

Dean had noticed nothing, thank heaven. Either that, or her reaction was purely internal. The last thing she needed was to have anyone guess how Reece Harland affected her—himself especially. Whatever it took, she had to face it out.

The seat he took was directly in line with her own, if several tables away. Lisa made no attempt to avoid the grey glance when he lifted his head from his study of the menu. Coffee-cup in hand, she returned his gaze steadily for a lengthy moment before turning without haste to address the younger man seated at right angles to her, conscious as she was of the tension in her stomach muscles. Detest Reece Harland as a person though she might, she was vitally aware of him as a man: that much she couldn't deny. He knew it too. His kind would.

He was still alone when, her own breakfast finished and arrangements still to be checked, she could no longer

put off the moment of departure. Bidding farewell to
Dean, who was in no hurry now that he had the whole
day to himself, she steeled herself to walk past the other
table without any outward sign of unease, even managed
a cool nod of recognition when he looked up at her.

'See you on board the *Tahoe Queen*,' he said easily,
bringing her to a reluctant but necessary halt.

'Do I take it both you *and* Miss Bellman will be coming
on the cruise?' she asked.

His shrug was a disclaimer. 'You'll have to ask her.
She hasn't surfaced yet.'

'We'll be gathering at the pier no later than ten-fifteen,'
Lisa said, ignoring the injunction. 'I have to make a head
count before we board in order to comply with
regulations.'

'Very commendable.' Being at a lower level in no way
displaced the air of authority in his manner. 'Glad to
see you taking things to heart.'

His return of attention to the food still in front of him
dismissed her more effectively than any words. Seething
inwardly, she went on her way. So far as he was concerned, last night might never have happened. There had
been no hint of it in his expression. The best thing she
could do was to forget it herself.

Except that wasn't going to be easy, came the sneaking
thought, when the very sight of him was all it took to
send her emotions haywire.

Those same emotions underwent a further dis-
arrangement two hours later when he turned up at the
pier with Sandra Bellman firmly in tow. The woman was
wearing a pair of scarlet trousers and toning silk shirt,
with totally unsuitable high-heeled sandals on her feet.

Lisa briefly contemplated pointing out the risk of a
sprained or even broken ankle resulting from catching

one of those heels in the deck boards, but discarded the idea in the almost certain knowledge that the advice would not be welcomed. If Reece Harland himself wasn't prepared to make the gesture, why should she worry? She took care to keep her expression strictly neutral when she caught his eye while making her count.

The *Tahoe Queen* was built in the style of one of the old river boats, powered by a huge paddle wheel at the stern. Painted in blue and white, and festooned with rainbow-hued bunting, it boasted three decks, the upper one of which was open to the elements. Boarding took time because of the contract photographer snapping each separate party in turn, but they were entertained by a banjo player dressed in appropriate Dixieland costume while they waited in line.

All very well done, Lisa thought, with typical American sparkle. So different from some of her previous side-trip experiences!

Most of her own party elected for the upper deck. The seats up there were soon taken, but no one seemed to mind standing. Preferring to see where they were going rather than where they'd been, Lisa found herself a good viewing spot up towards the bows, leaning both elbows on the white iron rail to gaze out at the surpassingly lovely backdrop of snow-capped mountains and pine forest.

North along the shore could be seen the cluster of taller buildings forming the commercial sector. Little Las Vegas by the Lake, she'd heard it called. She wondered idly if Dean were planning on more gambling today. It depended, she supposed, on the inclinations of his new girlfriend.

They got underway smoothly, backing out from the pier to turn about and head towards the south-western shoreline some miles distant. The breeze created by their passage was wonderfully fresh and stimulating. Lifting her face into it, Lisa mentally blessed the new hairstyle for its ease of attention. She was going to enjoy this three-hour sojourn, regardless of the paperwork to be completed at the end of it.

The Fullers were seated some short distance away. At least, the parents were—the two younger members didn't appear to be around. Lisa abandoned any idea she might have had of spending the three hours viewing scenery when Mrs Fuller beckoned to her. This, after all, was what she was here for.

'Ben's gone off sulking somewhere,' the woman confided. 'He didn't want to come on the cruise. June went to look for him, but I thought if you happened to see him, you might have a word with him. He'd listen to you.'

'He's got a crush on you,' declared her husband baldly. 'Blushes like a girl every time he lays eyes on you. Tell him to jump through hoops and he'll do it.'

'He's hardly going to come to any harm on board the *Queen*,' Lisa replied, turning a deaf ear to the rest. 'He looks sensible enough.'

Mr Fuller laughed. 'You don't know him! Totally unpredictable, that's Ben. Always was.'

'Then perhaps you should go and find him yourself,' she suggested with delicate emphasis. 'I mean, if you're worried about him...'

'I'm not the one doing the worrying,' he denied. 'He can't stay tied to the apron strings forever.'

Shades of a parental dispute there, thought Lisa, and one in which she had no intention of becoming involved. 'I'll keep my eyes open,' she promised, and moved away before anything else could be said.

A small bar set up alongside the bridge housing was serving drinks and cold snacks. She bought herself an iced orange juice, and moved aft to drink it. Other members of her group smiled and waved, but left her alone. Apart from the banjo player now serenading the decks, she appeared to be the only single ticket passenger on board. For the first time she began to feel the lack of a companion with whom to share the day.

She was standing in a corner of the deck watching the gulls soaring and swooping in the wake of the boat when Reece Harland spoke just behind her. His closeness jangled every nerve in her body.

'Enjoying the trip?'

'If you're hinting,' she said without turning, 'that I'm neglecting my duties again, I might point out that I'm on view and readily available to anyone who needs me.'

'So I see.' He moved to lean an elbow on the rail at her side, his mouth twisting a little as he glanced down at her. 'Problem is, knowing where to look.'

'I can't be everywhere at once,' she defended.

'True,' he agreed, 'but there are supposed to be two of you. What happened to... Dean, isn't it?'

Lying didn't come easily to her, but neither did letting down an associate. 'He wasn't feeling too well,' she said. 'A boat trip wouldn't have done him any good at all.'

'He seemed fine at breakfast.'

'So perhaps the food upset him.' The hands clasping the iron rail were white-knuckled. 'Do you make a habit of this kind of thing?'

'If you mean, do I poke my nose into everything, the answer is, only where it concerns me directly. I'm——'

'I know—a paying customer.' Her tone was flat. 'Don't worry, Mr Harland, I'll accord you the deference due.'

'That wasn't what I was about to say,' he returned evenly, 'but we'll let it stand. You've a way of making me lose sight of the main objective.'

And they both knew what *that* was, reflected Lisa sourly. 'Where did you leave Miss Bellman?' she asked with deliberation, and saw by the narrowing of the grey eyes that the dig had gone home. 'Won't she be feeling neglected?'

'She's gone below,' he said. 'The wind was messing her hair.' His eyes lifted to the spray-dampened thickness of her own, taking on some indefinable expression in the process. 'A regular nature girl yourself, I see.'

'I've neither time nor inclination for beauty salons,' she retorted crisply, stung, despite herself, by the intimation.

Lacking in mockery for once, his smile altered his whole face. 'I guess you don't have quite the same need.'

He was moving away again before she could come up with any response to what had been close to a compliment. She watched him go, her stomach muscles taut as bow strings.

Other eyes followed him too, she noted: all of them female, not all of them young. 'A man's man, a woman's ideal'—where had she read that quote? Except that he wasn't *her* ideal. Not when it came to personality. He was far too much the dominant male.

They were into the protected waters of the lovely Emerald Bay before she came across Ben Fuller. He was gazing morosely across at the ruins of what must once have been one of the world's tiniest churches, perched atop a rugged little island.

'I wonder why it was built there and not on the mainland,' she said lightly, joining him at the rail.

'Don't know,' he mumbled. His face had gone red again, although not quite so hot as last time.

'And not really all that interested.' Lisa took care to keep her tone casual. 'Can't say I blame you. Did you see your sister? She was looking for you.'

'She's over there somewhere, with a boy.' He sounded as if there was nothing unusual in *that*. 'She wasn't looking for me, just wanted to get out of Mum's sight and have some fun on her own.'

'Is that why you went off on your own too?' she asked, and saw the thin young shoulders hunch.

'This is a rotten holiday!' he burst out. 'We were supposed to be going to Florida, but Mum said everybody did that and she wanted something different. Now I'll never get to see Epcot!'

'We'll be spending three nights in Los Angeles,' Lisa reminded him. 'You'll be able to visit Disneyland there.'

'That's kid's stuff! I'm fourteen, not six!'

'Universal Studios, then. That's supposed to be really good.'

He glanced at her and away again, fair skin too tell-tale. 'Do you like your job?'

The question took her by surprise. 'I suppose I must,' she said, 'or I wouldn't be doing it.'

'I'm going to be a courier too after I get through school,' he confided. 'It's a whole lot better than sitting around in an office all day.'

'It's a whole lot different from being on holiday too. There's a ton of paperwork, and a great deal of responsibility—and you'll need to be fluent in at least one other language. On the other hand, it does offer a wide experience.' Lisa paused. 'How do you think your parents would feel about it?'

'Mum wouldn't like it. Not if it's going to take me away. Dad doesn't care what I do.'

'I'm sure that's not true.'

'Yes, it is.' The flatness of tone rejected any further debate. 'I'd better go back. Mum will be having kittens with both of us missing.' He pushed away from the rail, careful not to meet Lisa's gaze full on. 'See you.'

Lisa stayed where she was. She felt desperately sorry for the boy, but there was little she could do to help him through his teenage turmoil. Not in two weeks. Interference of any kind could only serve to worsen the situation. She had learned that fact of life very early on.

Storm clouds were spreading out from the mountains backing their home base when they emerged from the bay. Jagged forks of lightning streaked the dark mass.

'We're gonna meet that little lot head on!' declared a man close by where Lisa was standing. 'Let's get below before everybody gets the same idea.'

The upper deck gradually emptied as the clouds spread out across the sky, although the main force of the storm seemed to be centred over the mountains. Lisa went below when the first stinging drops of rain began to hit the deck, to find a crush through which it was difficult to pass. Not that anyone seemed too perturbed. Holiday spirit abounded.

Reece Harland was seated with his lady-love near the gangway on the long banquette seating running around the perimeter of the saloon. He beckoned Lisa over, standing up when she reached the spot to offer her his seat with an expression in his eyes that dared her to refuse.

Sandra looked daggers drawn—Lisa could feel the animosity coming from her in waves. She refused to allow it to bother her. The woman had first, last and whatever other claim she cared to try for.

Under pressure from the throng at his back, Reece was forced to stand up close—so close that one of his bare knees kept brushing against hers. Lisa was shocked by the sudden, almost overwhelming urge to reach out and touch the strong brown thigh, to feel the ripple of muscle beneath her fingers. Was one contemptuous kiss all it took to undermine principle? She didn't even like the man, for God's sake!

The movement of the boat had increased over the last few minutes as the surface of the lake roughened. A sudden roll to starboard had everyone staggering off balance, held on their feet only by the sheer volume of people in the place. Reece supported himself against the crush by sticking both hands up flat to the bulkhead above Lisa's head, but for a second or two she was within an inch of having her face buried in his midriff. She caught the clean, masculine scent of him, faint but emotive, and was aware of a rising heat deep inside. There was no controlling purely involuntary response, she acknowledged wryly. What she had to do was learn to ignore it.

'Sorry about that,' he said, straightening again as the pressure let up. 'Did I hurt you?'

She shook her head, not trusting her voice. He was too knowledgeable not to recognise her reaction, but that didn't mean she had to advertise it. Once off this boat she was going to make darned sure there was no physical contact between them again.

From the look on her face, Sandra would be mounting a campaign of her own. That she was by no means certain of her man was becoming daily more obvious. Men like Reece Harland took what they wanted, when they wanted, and went on their way untouched. Lisa could almost feel sorry for the woman.

The storm centre had receded back into the mountains again by the time they docked, the rain just about stopped. Developed while they were on the lake, the photographs were ready and waiting, pinned up on a board where people could pick out their own.

Expensive as always, Lisa saw, but just about everyone was buying regardless. Except for Reece and Sandra, that was. They'd been two of the few who had refused to have the photograph taken. Which only served to firm her suspicions. It was even possible that they were both of them married, although it was difficult to imagine the kind of woman *he* would consider worthy of his name.

She was becoming bitter and twisted, she told herself severely at that point, and it had to stop. Just do the job and forget everything else, that was the only way.

With the sun out again, and a lack of commitment, she spent the afternoon in and around the hotel pool. Heated to a comfortable seventy degrees, it attracted a number of guests. Lisa was sprawled on a lounger reading the latest Wilbur Smith, which she had picked up in the lobby shop, when Reece Harland put in an appearance at about three-thirty. He came over to take a chair from the nearby table and join her.

'Your back needs oiling again,' he said without preamble, 'or it's going to burn. What are you using?'

'I'm not,' she admitted reluctantly. 'I forgot to bring any lotion down with me. In any case, I'll be going in soon.'

Grey eyes took on the familiar mockery. 'Not on my account, I hope.'

'On account of the fact that I've been out here most of the afternoon already,' she returned with control.

'So take advantage of the rest. It may be the last chance you get.' He picked up the sun oil bottle he had brought with him, coming to take a seat on the edge of the lounger. 'I'll do the honours. Just lie still.'

Short of rolling off the other side of the lounger, she had little choice but to submit to his ministrations. Protestation of any kind would only serve to underline her reluctance to have him near her. She stifled a gasp at the cold trickle of the oil down her spine, gritting her teeth to the feel of his hands smoothing it out across her skin.

The sensation was exquisite, each and every movement a torment. Her one-piece, halter-necked suit was cut extra low in the back for maximum exposure. He went all the way down, covering every inch of skin with the long slow strokes, making her quiver inside where it didn't show.

'Miss Bellman isn't going to like this,' she said, fighting the inclination to tell him to stop, because that would be too much of a give-away.

'Miss Bellman isn't here,' he returned imperturbably. 'Not that it would matter.' He got to his feet to recap the bottle. 'That should do it. You can't be too careful of the sun at this altitude. The air temperature makes the strength deceptive.'

Lisa turned her head to look up at him, and wished she hadn't. The swimming trunks he was wearing left no doubt at all of his masculinity—if there had ever been any to start with. Her pulse-rate had gone into overdrive. Damn the man! Why couldn't he leave her alone?'

'Thanks,' she said gruffly. 'I'm sure I'll be fine now.'

The hint was ignored. Leaving the chair where it was, pulled up at the side of her lounger, he crossed the strip of concrete to take a header into the pool. Most of the other bathers had left by now. There was nothing to mar his swift progress from one end of the pool to the other, and back again. Not showing off, Lisa decided judiciously, watching him despite herself; he was simply exercising that superbly fit body.

There was little enough of the latter to be obtained on a tour of this nature, she was bound to admit. One seized one's chances where they occurred. For herself, she preferred the privacy of the early morning before anyone else was up and about, but he, no doubt, had better things to do with his time.

The whereabouts of Sandra Bellman right now was something of a puzzle in itself. She was hardly of an age where she would need an afternoon rest. The whole relationship was still uncertain, if it came to that. For a man supposedly enjoying an ilicit two weeks with his mistress, Reece displayed a singular lack of adherence.

As if in direct response to the thought, the blonde-haired American came into view on a second-floor balcony of the hotel a hundred yards or so away. Lisa resisted the temptation to put up a hand and wave to her as Reece Harland lifted himself from the water and came to seize his towel from the chair where he had left it draped.

'That water is overheated,' he observed, towelling moisture from this shoulders with a vigorous movement.

'Probably with young children in mind,' responded Lisa expressionlessly. 'They don't move as fast as you do.'

'Studying form, were you?' His tone was amused. 'How about showing me what *you* can do?'

'I'm covered in oil,' she retorted without moving. 'I'm hardly going to transfer that into the water.'

'Another time, then.'

Lisa kept her head down as he lowered himself into the chair. Extended, his lower legs and feet were in her line of vision. Good feet for a man, she found herself thinking: less sinewy than most, and lacking any sign of roughened skin. Whether the innuendo in those latter remarks had been intentional or not, she wasn't at all certain. Not that it mattered either way, because she had no intention of taking up the challenge.

The clicking of high heels across the forecourt was an early warning. Reece himself made no move. Stealing a glance, Lisa saw he had his hands clasped behind his neck in an attitude of total relaxation, his eyes closed against the glare from the lowering sun. The hair on his chest still glistened with droplets of water, like diamonds strung on curls of black wire. Ridged beneath tanned skin, the muscles of his stomach moved faintly in time with his breathing. He was all male, and infinitely disturbing. Too much so for any peace of mind.

Sandra Bellman was wearing a turquoise bikini that barely covered her vital areas. Narrow-eyed and taut-mouthed, she looked anything but lover-like.

'I thought we were supposed to be coming down to the pool together,' she accused the recumbent figure. 'I've been waiting up there like this for more than half an hour!'

'I was under the impression we were meeting down here,' Reece returned easily. 'Seems we were at cross-purposes. Do you want a lounger?'

'There's a couple already set up together over there,' came the pointed reply. 'You can't be very comfortable on that chair.'

'I was,' he said, without particular inflection. 'I'll fetch one over.'

'You can have mine,' offered Lisa, sitting up to reach for her wrap. 'I want to wash my hair before dinner.'

'I wouldn't have thought it took that long,' observed Reece.

'No, it doesn't.' She left the two of them to make what they liked of that remark, gathering up her things to depart with a nod and smile and a murmured, 'Have a nice day!'

Back in her room, she took a hot shower to get rid of the oil, emerging pink and tingling but somehow depressed. Her hair was dry enough to take a comb to by the time she finished towelling her body. Standing naked in front of the full-length mirror to restore order to the style, she found herself comparing her own slender curves with those of the American woman, and coming out the loser on all points.

So what? she asked herself emphatically. The kind of man attracted to voluptuousness in the female form was hardly going to be her type to start with. Take Reece Harland as a case in point. Whatever physical reactions he managed to arouse in her, he was far from being a man towards whom she could feel anything in the emotional sense.

CHAPTER FOUR

THEY left Tahoe at nine o'clock the following morning, heading across the state line to take the steep and winding road leading up and over Daggett Pass at nearly seven and a half thousand feet.

Across the flat and fertile valley beyond was the road which would take them almost a hundred miles down to Lee Vining, from where they would cut west through the Sierra Nevada to Yosemite. Between then and now, Lisa knew from her study of the area, lay a scenic wilderness only occasionally interrupted by civilisation.

Dean had been visibly under the weather this morning. She had heard him come into his room around four, which went some way towards explaining his condition. At least there should be no more distractions of that nature until they hit Vegas in two days' time.

Her own distractions were more immediate. Try as she might, it was impossible to turn a blind eye to Sandra Bellman's unconcealed animosity. Reece seemed unaware of it. Either that, or he considered it part of her job to grin and bear with whatever was thrown at her. Responding to an icily sarcastic request for some *decent* coffee, Lisa had to bring all her self-control to bear in order to stop herself from speaking her mind. How any man could find a shrew like this one attractive was beyond all reason!

Except that Sandra's attitude towards Reece was hardly the same, of course, so why should he care?

Ben Fuller offered comfort in the shape of a shy but sympathetic smile every time she passed his seat. He had given up arguing with his sister over turns at the window, and seemed content to just sit and watch Lisa going about her business. Her occasional commentary on passing areas of particular interest was received with rapt attention. He even took notes, which was more than anyone else did. Perhaps fortunately, his sister was too engrossed in her magazine to notice his attachment. She had already shown herself singularly lacking in sensitivity.

Requests by several people for photographic stops were given due consideration. They were far enough ahead of schedule to allow half an hour, Barry agreed, and he knew the ideal spot for the best shots.

He used the CB to call up Don Jackson, the other driver, who was bringing up the rear. Shortly afterwards, the two coaches pulled in to a cleared area on the edge of the forest, with a stupendous view of range after range of mountains fading into the far distance.

The air up here was deliciously cool, the scent of pine so strong it ousted everything else. With the occupants of both coaches mingling, and Dean in proximity, Lisa saw no harm in taking a short stroll along one of the narrow trails leading off from the clearing. Anything just to be on her own for a few minutes.

Seeing the flash of yellow through the trees some distance ahead, she came to the conclusion that someone else had had the same idea. Whoever it was, they were going in too deep for the time they had available.

So far as she could recall, the only person wearing yellow on her coach that day was June Fuller, although there had been a man on the other coach with a yellow shirt. Far more likely, Lisa thought, that it would be him. Not that it made much difference who it was in the long run. Getting them back was what mattered.

She tried calling out, but gained no response except from the birds in the vicinity. Thankful of the flat-heeled sandals, she put on a spurt, but the going was becoming rougher, the trail itself beginning to merge into the tinder-dry undergrowth. One careless match would be all it took to set light to this little lot, Lisa realised, and hoped that the person up ahead wasn't a smoker.

It was a further five minutes before she managed to catch up with her quarry, and only then because the latter had paused to gaze at something in the denser under-brush on the far side of the small clearing.

'You scared it!' accused the girl in the yellow shorts and top. 'What are you following me for, anyway? I don't need looking after!'

'Scared what?' asked Lisa, ignoring both question and statement.

'A bear cub. At least, that's what it looked like.' The pretty face was set in lines of discontent. 'It's bad enough having my mother keeping tabs on me all the time without you doing it too!'

'As a matter of fact, I was taking a breather away from you all when I spotted you up ahead.' Lisa was trying to keep her tone level. 'If that was a bear cub you saw, the mother can't be far away. We'd better get back.'

The black look was taken over by dawning alarm as the warning penetrated. June cast a suddenly nervous glance into the shadows of the thickly crowding trees. 'I didn't think about that!'

Turning to start back the way they had come as the girl joined her, Lisa hesitated. From where she stood it was almost impossible to discern any pathway. The trees themselves seemed to have closed in behind her.

Providing she had turned a full one hundred and eighty degrees, she should now be facing in the right direction, but it all looked the same.

Filtering through the canopy above, the sun seemed to be almost directly overhead, so that was no help. She would simply have to rely on her instincts, and those told her to angle a little way to her left. If she was wrong, there was every possibility of wandering further and further into a forest which stretched for miles and held all kinds of hidden dangers.

June wasn't the only one guilty of lack of fore-thought, came the rueful acknowledgement. This was no place for a nature walk. Not without a proper woodsman in tow, at any rate. None of which helped their present predicament.

The loud hail ringing through the trees was a relief of the first water. Lisa called back, and began making in the direction of the sound, with June close at her heels.

It took several minutes to locate the source due to the echo created by the trees. Seeing Reece Harland standing there waiting for them gave her little pleasure.

'What the devil do you think you're playing at?' he demanded harshly. 'This isn't your English woodland, woman, it's virgin forest! You could have run into any-thing!' He switched his attention to the girl at Lisa's rear, brows black as thunder. 'Your mother's going to be worried to death by now—or doesn't that bother you?'

'It might be an idea if we saved the recriminations for later, and just concentrate on getting back,' put in Lisa before June could voice the sulky retort obviously trem-bling on her lips. 'It was foolish to wander so far, we're all agreed on that, but no harm done.' Green eyes refused to flinch away from furious grey ones. 'You seem to have the best sense of direction, so perhaps you'd lead?'

He turned abruptly to do so, leaving Lisa with the distinct impression that said recriminations would certainly be forthcoming. Just why he should consider himself qualified to extend them was a point she would be making when the time came. Grateful as she was for the intervention, she had no intention of allowing him to haul her over any further coals of fire.

They hit the trail again at a point a little lower down. Once within sight of the road and the parked coaches, Reece told the younger girl to go on ahead and make her peace with her parents.

'How did you know which way we'd gone?' asked Lisa, to forestall his intention.

'I saw *you* taking off,' he returned grimly. 'I didn't realise you were following somebody. It didn't, of course, occur to you to tell anyone else what was happening?'

'Only because I didn't realise there was anyone up ahead initially,' Lisa responded, trying to stay cool. 'By the time I did, it was too late to turn back. I had to keep them in sight.'

'And get yourself lost in the process.'

'We weren't lost,' she denied. 'I knew which way we'd come.'

'Sure you did.' He made no attempt to iron out the scepticism from his tone. 'It doesn't alter the fact that you were irresponsible enough to set off in there in the first place.'

'If I hadn't, no one would have known where to start looking for June,' she pointed out, 'so it was perhaps as well.' She was watching the ground, treading carefully so as not to trip and fall. 'While it was considerate of you to take the trouble of keeping an eye on me, I'd sooner you didn't in future. After all, you wouldn't want Miss Bellman to feel neglected.'

'Sandra has nothing to do with this,' he growled. 'And don't try telling me what I should or shouldn't do. You need an eye keeping on you.'

That brought her head up, and sharply. 'Meaning I'm not performing my job to your satisfaction?'

'Meaning you're capable of what might turn out to be dangerous misjudgement.'

They were within earshot of the people now boarding the coaches. Lisa bit off her retort, and went with forced smile to join her party, avoiding Sandra Bellman's glittering gaze.

'Sorry for the delay, folks,' she said. 'Next stop lunch.'

Looking thoroughly fed up, June was urged aboard by her mother, who paused to have a word with Lisa.

'I'm so sorry for the trouble my daughter caused by going off like that on her own,' she said. 'I'll be making sure she doesn't do anything like it again.'

Don't crowd her, Lisa wanted to advise, but she kept her own counsel. She was no more equipped to play the psychologist than Reece Harland was fitted to become her unofficial custodian.

The latter was conversing with Sandra Bellman a short distance away—if conversing was the right word for an almost purely one-sided dialectic. Reece's face was expressionless, his hands thrust into the side pockets of his shorts in an attitude that should have been casual but wasn't. If looks were anything to go by, the blonde-haired American was digging herself an early grave so far as their association went. The wonder was how they had ever got together in the first place.

The two of them were the last to board. Lisa turned to say something to her driver as they approached, making sure they were both safely up the steps and moving to their seats before swinging on board in their wake. She hadn't heard the last from Reece Harland, that was certain, but for the present she had other things to think about. Time enough when they reached Yosemite to consider just how she was going to deal with his officiousness.

The highest point of the whole tour at nearly ten thousand feet, the Tioga Pass also proved the most sensational. Lisa tended to close her eyes on some of the hairpin bends and put her trust in Barry's skill as a driver to get them through unscathed. No camera could capture the true magnificence of the white-capped peaks, she acknowledged, and after a while stopped even trying.

Yosemite itself was a broad, meadow-like valley surrounded by great domes and pinnacles of rock, and threaded by fast-running mountain streams. Too crowded at this time of year for Lisa's personal tastes, but a must on the itinerary.

They reached the hotel with several hours of daylight still in hand for those who wished to do some exploring on foot. Lisa opted for a little sunbathing on her own private veranda, soaking up the golden heat and the peace. In a country the size of this one, a great deal of time had to be spent on the road in order to see even a fraction of it over the course of two short weeks. Not a restful kind of holiday at all, but one not to be missed either.

This one trip was probably all she was going to get, she reminded herself wryly, so she had better make the most of it. Unless a miracle happened, she would be out of the country altogether by the end of the summer. What she couldn't contemplate was life here as an illegal alien, always in fear of discovery and deportation. She just didn't have what it took.

The knock on her room door came at around five-thirty when she was seriously contemplating a shower and an early dinner. Going to answer the summons in anticipation of finding one of the hotel staff outside with some query or other, she was totally nonplussed to see Sandra Bellman standing there in the corridor.

'I think it's time you and I had a talk,' declared the latter forcefully, advancing into the room without waiting for an invitation.

Short of shutting the door in her face, Lisa had no choice but to fall back before her. 'About what?' she asked, already aware of the answer.

'About the fact that Reece Harland is with me. If you know what's good for you, you'll steer well clear!'

'If I knew what was good for me I probably shouldn't even be here at all,' returned Lisa coolly. 'You might be better employed having a word with Mr Harland himself. He's the one doing the following.'

'To keep tabs on you, no other reason. That's what he's here for.'

Lisa stared at her in sudden and genuine bewilderment. 'I'm sorry?'

The blue eyes were malicious. 'As the man in charge of this end of the business, he's entitled to know how things are run. I can tell you now, he's in no way satisfied with this part of the organisation.'

'Just a minute.' Lisa held up a staying hand. 'Let me get this straight. You're saying he's here in an official capacity?'

'Got it in one!' The sarcasm was overdone. 'You think we'd either of us travel this way by choice? Reece believes in personal investigations when it comes to new acquisitions. And things aren't good, you can take my word for that. There's going to be one almighty shake-up of this company when we get back to base!'

Lisa was silent, mind going back over the past days. Things were beginning to click into place. A company take-over, Dean had said. To all intents and purposes, Reece Harland was here on no less than a spying mission to judge the quality of service. It explained so much about his whole attitude.

Anger boiled up in her. Of all the underhand methods to employ, this just about took the biscuit!

'I gather he doesn't know you were coming to see me,' she said silkily, 'so there's not much point in asking you to pass on a message for me. I'll tell him myself, to his face, what I think of his tactics.'

A shadow of doubt crossed the beautifully arranged features. 'You'll lose your job on the spot if you do.'

'I doubt it. Not unless he can be sure of picking up another courier en route.' Lisa added with deliberation, 'Or perhaps you might fancy taking over the job yourself?'

Delicate nostrils pinched. 'I'm no uniformed menial!'

'No, that I can definitely go along with.' A spirit of recklessness had overtaken Lisa. With no permanent position at risk, she could afford to speak her mind. 'You don't have the disposition to help anyone but yourself. Now, if you wouldn't mind leaving, please, I'd like to have a shower.'

'You'll be sorry,' warned the other wrathfully. 'Just see if I'm right!'

'I'll take a chance on it.' Lisa was past caring about anything right now but getting this woman out of her room. 'Good*bye*, Miss Bellman!'

Closing the door on the retreating figure, she leaned her weight against it for a moment to contemplate what

she had learned. Reece Harland's methods left a whole
lot to be desired in every sphere, though she supposed
he had right on his side so far as the actual business was
concerned. What really stuck in her throat was the fact
of his bringing Sandra along as a diversion, because it
was suddenly obvious that that was all she was. The
separate rooms enabled him to take advantage of her
presence when he felt like it, but gave him plenty of scope
to pursue any other interest that might come his way.

She herself came under that heading; she was suddenly sure of that too. His whole attitude towards her
was redolent of sexual pursuit. Anger mingled with some
other emotion she wasn't prepared to define. If that was
the kind of game he liked playing, so be it! There would
be some satisfaction to be gained by turning the tables
on him.

It was doubtful that Sandra would admit to having
given him away unless forced by her, Lisa's, subsequent
actions. And *she* had no intention of telling him. Not
yet, at any rate.

Showered, and dressed in lemon cotton trousers and
shirt, she went down at six-thirty to secure a table for
dinner. Dean came to join her a few minutes later.
Tonight he was wearing pale blue trousers with a deeper
toned shirt, and looked, Lisa was bound to acknowledge, devastatingly handsome. This job really
didn't do him justice, she thought. His face was his
fortune.

'Did you never consider trying your luck in LA?' she
asked casually over the melon cocktail chosen by them
both for first course.

His laugh was short. 'Sure. Along with thousands of
others. I'm just not geared to standing in line.'

'I shouldn't have thought,' she ventured, 'that you'd found your ideal niche doing what you are doing either.'

'Oh, I guess it has its compensations.' His glance shifted to a spot beyond her shoulder as he spoke, a smile playing about his lips. 'Unexpected ones, sometimes.'

About to ask him what he meant, Lisa felt the words dry on her lips as she saw Reece Harland come through the swing-doors from the lobby. Sandra was with him, of course, and viewing her surroundings with her customary disdain.

Catching Lisa's eye across the room, she swiftly looked away again, though not in time to stop the flash of pure antagonism from winging forth. Coming to warn her off that way had been a mistake, and the woman knew it. All she had done was underline her own lack of certainty where her lover was concerned.

Reece himself, Lisa saw through newly opened eyes. Casually dressed as he was in trousers and shirt, he still bore a certain, unmistakable stature. She should have guessed what he was from the word go: it wasn't the first time she had experienced a similar situation, although it was more common practice to dispatch an underling to do the sussing out.

It wasn't until they were seated three tables away that Reece allowed his gaze to travel around the room. Lisa made no attempt to look away as their eyes met, although she could feel the sudden thud of her heart against her ribcage. Her smile was slow and challenging—an unspoken invitation. The faint lift of one dark eyebrow was recognition enough: message received and understood.

I'm going to teach you a lesson, *Mr* Harland, she thought with emphasis. See how you like being on the receiving end for once!

Dean made no attempt to enlist her company to while away the rest of the evening. Persuasion, it appeared, was not to be contemplated. She should warn him about the spy in camp, came the thought, yet there was reluctance. For what these people were paying, they deserved full and proper service, and Dean simply wasn't giving it. According to one conversation Lisa had overheard, he didn't even bother to make coffee on board the coach—nor to volunteer information about places of interest unless specifically asked. His main concern seemed to be having as good a time as he could manage for the least effort.

Before leaving the dining-room after finishing her meal, she paused for a brief exchange with the Fullers, who she hadn't realised were seated right behind her. June seemed to have gained a whole new lease of life since the morning's episode. Her eyes were sparkling, her face all the prettier for the upward curve of her lips.

'Dean took a group of us up to see the Bridal Veil falls earlier,' said Mrs Fuller. 'Such a nice young man, giving up his time like that.'

'Yes, isn't he?' Lisa caught the suddenly heightened colour in June's face, and knew a sinking suspicion. Unexpected compensations, he had said a little while ago. But surely even he would stop short of playing around with a young girl's emotions?

No, he wouldn't, came the answer. Not if it provided him with the kind of attention his ego needed so badly. June Fuller might be young, but unattached girls were in short supply at the moment. She would have to keep a close eye on him these next couple of days until they reached Vegas.

She went out for a walk around the village before everything closed down for the night, to find herself part of a veritable throng drawn from the hotels and campsites providing accommodation in the valley. This was only a small part of the park, much of which could only be reached on foot or horseback.

She would have liked to do some trekking herself, but their schedule didn't allow for it. Tomorrow, they would be heading back over the pass and down to the place called Lone Pine, where they would spend the night before going into Death Valley the following day. She was looking forward to that experience, despite all the harrowing tales she had heard of the intense heat and constant dehydration.

By nine-thirty she had all her paperwork up to date and was able to retire to bed with Wilbur Smith. When she finally put out the light, it was still barely eleven.

Sleep came almost at once, deep and seemingly dreamless: at least, she couldn't recall dreaming when she awoke. It wasn't yet dawn, she realised, although the sky was beginning to turn a lighter shade of grey along the eastern rim.

Further sleep appeared to be out of the question. She had never felt wider awake. The urge to get up and do something grew in her until she had to obey it. If she went down to the pool now she could watch the sunrise. In such surroundings as these, that in itself had to be a spectacle worthy of note.

All was silent outside. Lisa shivered a little in the fresh morning air, but the pool was heated and welcoming. Sliding into the water as quietly as she could, she struck out in a slow and measured breast-stroke to swim the length of the pool, conscious of the sheer delight in being all alone. This might be the last time she had such opportunity, and she meant to make the most of it.

She had paused for a breather after several lengths when she first became aware of some other presence. The eastern sky was streaked with gold and pink, casting enough light for her to make out the figure seated on one of the loungers at the far end of the pool. As if in direct response to the recognition, Reece got up and dived in, creating scarcely a splash on entry and little noise from his passage towards her.

'Seems I wasn't the only one who couldn't sleep,' he commented on reaching her.

'The early bird catches the worm,' she responded blandly. 'It's going to be another lovely day by the feel of it.'

'Only the English would have any doubt this time of year,' he mocked. Judging by the glint in his eyes, the former comment had not gone unnoted. 'How long have you been down here?'

Arms spread along the rail at her back for support, Lisa shrugged. 'Fifteen minutes, maybe. I wasn't counting.' His closeness was a goad to the emotions rising in her. She wanted to lash out at him, to tell him exactly what she thought of his methods. The only thing holding her back was the desire to retaliate in kind. She could give him a run for his money, if nothing else.

'I love the early morning,' she added, adopting a softer note. 'It's the best part of the day.'

'Depends what you're doing with the rest of it,' he came back smoothly. 'Considering your job, I guess you're right.'

'As a matter of fact, I enjoy the job. It's an opportunity to travel——' the slight pause was calculated '—and meet people.'

'*En masse*, or individually?'

'Both.' Broad and powerful, his naked shoulders made her fingers itch to touch and feel. The muscle structure was that of a gymnast, beautifully honed. From her contact with him the other night, she already knew the strength in those rippling biceps.

'You keep yourself very fit,' she commented, and didn't have to inject the sudden husky quality into her voice. 'A regular Mr Universe!'

Something flickered deep down in the grey eyes. He put both hands on her hips, holding her still as he moved closer. His lips were teasing, playing with hers in tiny nibbling kisses that roused her to respond in kind.

Her breath had shortened, her pulse-rate increased to a point where she thought the delicate skin at her temples might rupture beneath the pressure. Any idea she had entertained of keeping a level head was swiftly vanishing. What she wanted was for this to go on and on—for his hands to move over her skin, finding all those fluttering, tremoring nerve-points.

Without considering the outcome, she slid both arms about his neck to bring herself up closer against him, thrilling to the feel of the lean, hard body. His mouth had stopped teasing and become demanding, pressuring her lips apart with a purposefulness that brooked no rejection. Lisa felt the *frisson* run through her entire body at the first probing touch of his tongue. She clung to him in an ecstasy of sensation, responding to an urge spreading from the very centre of her being to every corner of her body.

CHAPTER FIVE

LISA'S one-piece suit was held up only by a narrow halter strap. The feel of the water against her bare breasts when Reece drew the covering material down to her waist was as nothing compared to the wiry tingle of his body hair against her swollen, aching nipples. She gasped and arched her back, bringing the lower half of her body into even closer contact with the hard readiness of his— hearing his muttered exclamation.

Only then, as he began to peel the suit down over her hips, did she finally come to her senses. Desperation lent her the strength to pull away from him and make for the steps a short distance away, tugging the suit back up into place as she went.

He caught her before she was halfway out of the pool, clamping two hands like vices about her waist to yank her down and round again. The steadily growing light revealed a face as hard as nails and eyes like gimlets.

'I'm not sure what game you think you're playing, but you chose the wrong partner,' he gritted.

'It's no game.' Her voice tremored. 'I never intended it to happen.'

His laugh was humourless. 'Like hell you didn't! You were giving out more signals than a navy flagship! There's a name for women like you. Crude but appropriate. Want to hear it?'

Anger as memory returned freed her from the restraint put on her tongue. 'There's a name for people like you too. Try hypocrite for size!'

Dark brows drew together. 'What's that supposed to mean?'

'Think about it.' Despite the controlled temperature of the water, she was shivering. 'Are you going to let me go or do I have to start screaming rape?'

'Try it,' he invited, 'and you'll have something to scream about. You don't go anywhere until you tell me what all this is about.'

It was too late to retract, Lisa acknowledged without particular regret. She needed some kind of axe to grind in order to forget how close she had come to disaster. The imprint of his lips and body still lingered, making her tremble deep down. There was an aching sense of loss.

'I know who you really are,' she said tautly. 'That should be answer enough. If it weren't for the fact that I'd be leaving Dean with an impossible situation, I'd tell you what you could do with the job here and now!'

'Sure you would.' There was no lessening of hardness in his voice. 'So you know who I am. You didn't learn it over the last few minutes, so why the come-on?'

'There was no come-on.' She said it between her teeth. '*You* kissed *me*, not the other way round!'

'I kissed you because you were making it obvious that was what you wanted. The rest was mutual.' He wasn't giving an inch. 'You've a strange way of showing disapproval.'

'It wasn't meant——' She broke off, biting her lip.

'Wasn't meant to go that far?' Reece supplied. 'So I gathered. Rouse the swine and leave him aching—was that the plan?'

Lisa tried to steady her voice. 'It's immaterial now. If you don't mind, I'd like to go back to my room.'

His own voice came soft but by no means gentle. 'Not before you pay a few more dues.'

She struggled as he drew her up to him again, but it was like fighting a brick wall. His mouth was ruthless, his hands sliding down to seize her buttocks and bring her into even closer proximity, making her aware of every muscular line of his lean, hard body.

Emotions at war, she forced herself to be still and unresponsive. The sun was coming up in a haze of glory; she could see the glow through her closed lids. Other early risers might soon be around. They mustn't find them here like this!

As if in direct response to the thought, he let her go, thrusting her away from him with a muttered exclamation.

'We'll sort this out later,' he said, 'when we've both cooled down.'

'There's nothing to sort.' She was climbing from the water as she said it, putting distance between them. 'I'll do my job while you concentrate on keeping Miss Bellman happy!'

He hoisted himself on to the edge in one strong surge, blocking her way with an arm stretched across the upper handrail. 'Let's get one thing straight,' he clipped. 'I'm not Sandra Bellman's keeper, any more than she's mine.'

Conscious of the downward creep of the unsecured suit top, Lisa fought to stop herself from clutching at it. 'She doesn't appear to share that opinion.'

'Tough.'

'You really don't give a damn for anyone, do you?' she burst out savagely. 'You dragged her out here——'

'Correction. She booked herself on this trip.' His tone was sardonic. 'Why else do you imagine we'd be occupying different rooms?'

That stopped her, but only for a moment. 'She must have had good reason to believe her company would be welcomed. Anyway, she isn't the issue, is she?'

'Isn't she?' Grey eyes took on a mocking gleam at the swift run of colour under her skin. 'I'm not sleeping with her, if that's what's concerning you.'

'I couldn't care less,' she lied, 'who or what you sleep with! What does concern me is your low-down way of going about this whole affair.'

He shrugged. 'I'm entitled to take a look at what goes on.'

'You could have done that without all the secrecy.'

'With everyone on their best behaviour? Not much point. As it is, I'm getting the true picture—and I'm not overly impressed.'

He was still blocking her exit from the water. Vulnerable in a suit only just covering her nipples, Lisa made a valiant attempt to restore the balance. 'I'll really try to do better.'

'For a temp, you're not doing too badly,' he responded. 'It's Price I'm talking about. He's more of a passenger than the ones paying for the privilege.'

She could hardly argue with that assessment. 'So you'll be giving him the elbow when we get back to base?'

'Depends how he shapes up from here on in.' He added on a sharper note, 'And no warnings from you either. So far as he's concerned, I'm still a paying passenger.'

'So far as *I'm* concerned,' she said tautly, 'you're still taking an unfair advantage. Why not get one of your underlings to do your dirty work?'

'Because I prefer occasional first-hand experience.'

He took the arm away from the rail, coming to his feet as she emerged at last on to the pool side. Barefooted, she was at a distinct disadvantage when it came to height. His chest was on a level with her eyes.

The sun was above the horizon now, its heat already drying her skin. There was movement and sound from the direction of the hotel, followed by the emergence on to the patio of a room cleaner's trolley piled high with fresh bed linen. The woman pushing it gave the two of them an incurious glance before disappearing into one of the locker-rooms.

'That suit isn't going to hold up much longer without a hoist,' commented Reece. 'Not that I'd object.'

'I'm sure of it.' Lisa picked up the towel she had left draped across the nearest lounger, and wrapped it about her shoulders. 'May I go now? We're supposed to be making an eight o'clock start.'

'By all means.'

He fell into step right behind her, picking up his own towel on the way. Lisa wanted to run from him, but pride forbade it. Her skin prickled to the memory of his exploring hands; she could feel her nipples pressing against the material, the deep-down ache of repression. If he touched her again she would find it impossible to conceal her feelings.

Her room was on the ground floor, his on the upper. As yet, there was no one else about.

'See you at breakfast,' he said, heading up the outside staircase. 'Don't be late.'

Lisa had left her door unlocked. Slipping inside, she caught sight of herself in the dressing-table mirror right opposite. Her hair looked a mess. She would have to shampoo it in the shower. At least she wasn't going to be short of time. It was still barely six.

What she was going to do about Dean, she wasn't at all sure. In one sense, he deserved whatever was coming to him, yet she still felt a certain loyalty.

Reece couldn't really expect her to keep silent; he didn't have any right to demand it of her. His own ethics hardly bore close examination. Even if it was true that Sandra had invited herself along on this trip in the hope of furthering their relationship, it didn't excuse his behaviour. Temporary though the position might well be, she, Lisa, was an employee of the company, and as such surely off limits.

Like most small towns along Route 395, Lone Pine was little more than a main street flanked by general stores, a garage, one or two fast food restaurants and a couple of motels.

They arrived at five after taking a scenic detour around the June Lake loop further back. The snow-caps had been left behind now, the mountain ridges golden in the afternoon sunlight. Alighting from the air-conditioned coach was like stepping in front of a furnace door. Even at this hour, the heat was fierce.

Tired after a long day's travelling, most people seemed glad to spend a quiet evening. A good thing, Dean remarked sourly over a substantial meal at one of the diners, as there was little else to do in this dead-end quarter.

'It's a handy place to start tomorrow's route from,' Lisa returned mildly, 'and there'll be more than enough entertainment in Vegas, I imagine. Is it really round the clock?'

'The gambling is.' He brightened at the thought. 'Two whole nights of it!'

'We're doing Hoover Dam as an optional extra on Friday,' Lisa reminded him. She paused, still torn by indecision over whether to pass on the warning or not. If Dean pulled his socks up only because he was being watched, then it still wasn't going to improve his future performance. On the other hand, could she simply stand by knowing he might well lose his job altogether if he remained in happy ignorance? It was a dilemma she could well have done without.

Reece had spent much of the travelling time today with his head back against the cushion and his eyes closed. Sitting for hours in a coach was obviously not his ideal vacation, no matter how stupendous the scenery. Poetic justice, Lisa thought. He deserved far worse than mere boredom for his sins.

She could almost feel sorry for Sandra, whose frustration was unconcealed. To make such an effort just to be with a man, and then get nowhere, must be galling in the extreme for a woman of her nature.

Apart from the tour party, there were few other people staying in the motel. Walking along the outside balcony to her room after leaving Dean to mooch around the town, Lisa noted a couple of people down by the small pool. It was only on reaching her door, which was almost directly above, that she realised who the couple were.

Reece was seated on the edge of Sandra's lounger, body angled towards her in unmistakable intimacy. They had neither of them eaten at the same place most of the party had used; there was every possibility, Lisa thought now, that they hadn't bothered eating at all. A cooling swim after a heated session of lovemaking, perhaps? Even if Reece had been telling the truth concerning the woman's presence on the trip, which was by no means certain, it didn't mean he was against making the most of her being here.

Putting a name to the emotion threatening to choke her wasn't difficult, Lisa acknowledged ruefully. Detest and distrust Reece Harland though she might, she was irretrievably drawn to him. He knew it too. After this morning, he couldn't fail to know. One thing was certain, she couldn't afford to put herself in that position again. He was too ready to take advantage.

So far as temperature was concerned, Death Valley more than lived up to its name. What Lisa hadn't been prepared for was the sheer magnitude of the area. In places, the shimmering desert sands looked like vast stretches of water—a mirage the early settlers trekking through to California must have deplored.

Furnace Creek, where they stopped for lunch, provided a welcome spot of greenery in the shape of palm trees and grass. The information centre was staffed by people who lived all year round in the valley, emerging from it, Lisa was told by one woman, only once a month to make the journey to Las Vegas for essential supplies. They didn't miss the outside world at all, the woman assured her. She herself had been here more than ten years, and wouldn't dream of leaving.

'Rather them than me,' declared Dean when Lisa mentioned the matter. 'It must be like living with the aftermath of a nuclear war before it even happens!'

For once, Lisa could agree with his point of view. The valley had its own special kind of beauty, but the heat and lack of vegetation would soon pall. One had to keep up an almost constant liquid intake to combat dehydration.

Perusing the contents of the gift shop, she rounded a section of shelves to find Reece studying a book on Indian craftwork.

'My mother might like this,' he said casually. 'She's into jewellery design as a hobby.'

'Does she live in San Francisco too?' asked Lisa, torn between the urge to leave him standing there and common politeness.

He shook his head. 'Los Angeles. I'll be calling in on her while we're there.' There was a slight pause before he added, 'You might like to come and meet her.'

Surprise kept her speechless for a moment. When she did respond it was with asperity. 'Along with Miss Bellman? No, thanks!'

'Sandra will be leaving the tour at Vegas.' He said it without a flicker of expression. 'She has to get back.'

'Husband caught up with her?' The words were out before she could stop them.

He said levelly. 'A requirement of this job is to get your facts right. She isn't married. Neither, if it comes to that, am I. Chiefly because I've never met a woman capable of measuring up to *my* requirements.'

It was too late now to try retracting anything, Lisa decided. Too late, and too much like grovelling. 'That I can well believe,' she retorted crisply. 'Does such a person exist, I wonder?'

'I live in hope.' Another pause heralded a slight change of tone. 'Were you planning on staying on in the States?'

She picked up a small stone figure, turning it over to look at the price ticket stuck to the base. 'Only if I can do it legally.'

'I might be able to help you.'

Lisa replaced the figure carefully on the shelf before looking up at him. 'Why would you do that?'

He shrugged. 'Apart from the odd incident, you're good at your job.' The grey eyes moved over her face, taking on some new expression. 'It might help ease things between us for the rest of this tour too.'

Realisation was like an open-handed slap. She could hardly control the urge to reach out and perform the physical act on him. She said icily, 'I see. Be nice to you, and you'll see what you can do. Thank you, but I've no intention of filling in for Miss Bellman. If boredom is going to be a problem for you, I'm sure you can persuade her to stay on.'

The lean features scarcely altered expression, but there was no mistaking the slow inhalation of breath. 'I'm going to take a great deal of pleasure in fetching you down off that soapbox,' he said softly. 'Boredom won't come into it.'

'It takes two,' she said, and wondered at her ability to ignore the painful tension in her chest. 'You may be way up in the company hierarchy, but I'm not subject to any coercion. You can keep your offer. If I stay on in America it will be via my own efforts!'

'Unlikely.' The steel in his eyes was reflected by that in his voice. 'Hadn't you better get back to your duties? We're due to leave in about six minutes.'

Lisa turned with admirable restraint, and left him standing there. She was seething inside with more than mere anger. What kind of a fool did he think she was? His threats meant nothing because she had no intention of placing herself in a position where he could further his aim, but that didn't excuse them. His arrogant assumptions had no basis in fact.

They had some, came the small voice of reason. Her response to him this morning in the hotel pool had hardly been one of total uninterest. Steering clear of him was good all-round policy.

He was one of the last to return to the coach. Carrying a wrapped parcel which Lisa assumed was the book he had been looking at, he climbed aboard without a glance in her direction.

Sandra was already seated. Watching her greet the man taking his seat at her side, Lisa wondered cynically if she already knew about her impending departure. Not that there was any doubt in her mind that the woman would indeed be leaving the tour. If Reece wanted out, he would have her on the first available flight. How was something else again.

From Furnace Creek they took the Badwater route out from the valley. Standing by the shallow spread of undrinkable water, Lisa found it hard to believe that they were almost two hundred and eight feet below sea-level. It must have been a frightening experience, she thought, for the pioneers lost in Death Valley so long ago to look across the miles of desolate salt flats and barren hills. It had taken them nearly a month to find a way out. How they had existed that long, heaven only knew!

It was even hotter here than at the Centre. After just a few minutes, those who had ventured off the coaches were only too ready to climb aboard again and be on their way. Deposits of iron oxides in the rock formations produced a dozen different shades of red and violet, all overlaid with the silvered sparkle of mica. As the shadows began to lengthen, the desert itself took on colour, as if some unseen artist were slowly filling in the outline.

By four o'clock they had reached the point where the road began its steep-angled climb from the valley. As on the way in that morning, Barry was forced to switch off the air-conditioning in order to stop the engine from

overheating while making the climb. Saying goodbye to
this particular part of California was no great hardship,
Lisa reflected on reaching the top, although she wouldn't
have missed the experience. A further two hours or so
should see them in Las Vegas, with plenty of time in
which to recover from today's exertions.

Plenty of time also, came the intrusive thought, for
Reece Harland to do his worst. Keeping out of his way
wasn't going to be all that easy.

The gambling city proved more of everything that she
had ever imagined about it. Big, brash, and bustling, it
lay in the desert like a visitation from another planet.
Driving along the famous Strip was an experience so incongruous with what had gone before, it seemed unreal.

Their hotel lay just south of the main casino centre.
No less than six storeys, it was dwarfed by the towering
height and breadth of the Hilton a couple of blocks away.
There was a casino area inside, of course. Apart from
the churches, no public building in Las Vegas was
without at least a couple of fruit machines.

Allocation of rooms took quite some time owing to
the size of the incoming party. By the time Lisa had her
own key safely in her hand, it was already approaching
seven-thirty.

The view from her fifth-floor window made up for
the long wait to gain a space in a lift at this hour when
everyone, it seemed, was on the move. She could see the
Strip in both directions, alive with colour and flashing
design. A short distance north lay the vast floodlit curve
of Caesar's Palace, with its moving platform carrying
people from the pavement into its welcoming depths.
Beyond that again, the two huge palm trees of the
'Dunes' display shimmered and sparkled in endless
motion.

Not for the first time, Lisa felt the lack of someone to share it all with. Loneliness wasn't a new phenomenon. There had simply never been anyone she had cared enough about to want a serious, long-lasting relationship with. Since losing her parents, there hadn't been a man in her life at all.

One thing she did know, she reflected now. Reece Harland was not going to be her first affair. Involvement of that nature was the last thing she either wanted or needed.

There was little sign of the tour group at dinner. With so much going on outside, and so many places at which to eat along the way, it wasn't so surprising, Lisa conceded, that they would all of them want to make the most of it. She could conjure little enthusiasm herself. Where could a lone female go in a place like this without laying herself open to misinterpretation?

Reluctant to be alone in her room, she was writing up the daily report in the lobby when Reece came in through the revolving doors. He was wearing the same cream trousers and brown shirt in which he had travelled, and was in urgent need of a shave, she noted in some surprise. Not like him at all.

'I've yet to see Price fulfilling that requirement,' he said, pausing beside the sofa on which she was seated. 'It might be an idea to remind him.'

'I don't think I'm qualified to do that,' Lisa returned levelly, not looking at him.

'Even if it meant the difference between his keeping his job and losing it?'

That did bring her head up, and sharpish. 'Don't try to make me responsible for what happens. If you're that concerned for him, put him in the picture.'

'I didn't say I was concerned.' His tone was deceptively mild. 'Where is he, anyway?'

She made some attempt to regain her composure. 'Out on the town, I'd imagine, like everyone else.'

'Apart from yourself.'

Her shrug was meant to convey indifference. 'I'm no gambler.'

'You don't have to be to enjoy the spectacle.' He studied her for a moment, taking in the multi-hued cotton skirt and sleeveless top she had donned in an effort to cheer herself up. When he spoke again it was decisively. 'Give me fifteen minutes.'

Like hell she would! Lisa thought. Where Sandra Bellman had got to wasn't at all clear, but there was every possibility that the woman had already departed. Which left a gap she did not intend filling, either tonight or any other night. Hadn't she already made that clear?

Gathering up her things, she took the lift after Reece's. He was on the third floor, so there was no chance of running into him. She would wait an hour, then perhaps risk a stroll along the Strip just to look at the lights. The crowds out there were dense enough to make isolation next to impossible anyway.

Coming some twenty minutes later, the knock on her room door was too incisive for any mistake to be made. Lisa considered simply ignoring it, but a second and even firmer knock underlined the unlikelihood of his departure without fuss. Steeling herself, she went to open up.

There was calculation in the grey gaze. Changed into white trousers and dark green shirt, with his jaw smooth and smelling faintly of aftershave, he was no less of a threat.

'Running away?' he queried silkily. 'I didn't think you had it in you.'

'I came up here to finish my report in peace,' she retorted. 'I'd be grateful if you left me to do just that.'

'From what I saw, you'd already signed off,' he said. 'A few lines is all that's needed—unless something out of the ordinary run of things happens. Today was relatively uneventful, wouldn't you say?'

'And going to stay that way,' she countered, making to close the door again. 'Goodnight, Mr Harland.'

He stopped the advancing door with a strong push, forcing her to retreat as he came into the room. 'I'm not leaving you sitting around on your own,' he declared. 'You're coming out with me if I have to drag you!'

He was serious about it; she could see that. She said tensely, 'Is that your usual method?'

His smile was both fleeting and lacking in humour. 'I don't normally have to do any persuading. Supposing I make it an order? You're still officially on duty.'

Lisa searched his face, emotions in conflict. A part of her wanted suddenly and badly to go along, while another advised caution. Regardless of how she felt about him, the attraction he held for her was too insidious to be set aside.

'What about San...Miss Bellman?' she asked.

'I saw her on to a plane over an hour ago.'

She would have liked to ask why, but doubted if he would tell her. Whatever the relationship between the two of them, it obviously hadn't survived Sandra's surprise appearance on the tour. A bad mistake on her part.

'I'm no substitute,' she warned, and saw the corner of his mouth turn down.

'Agreed. Shall we go?'

CHAPTER SIX

LAS VEGAS by night was an eye-opener in every sense. Lisa lost track of the number of different casinos they visited. She was bemused by the sheer volume of people milling around the vast areas, by the clatter of coins hitting the metal trays, by the flashing lights and ringing bells announcing a minor jackpot somewhere amid the endless banks of machines.

She watched Reece play a few games of blackjack, and tried to follow the cards the way he was so obviously doing. The croupier was a girl about her own age whose smile was fixed if the game wasn't. Reece came out on top by a few dollars, which he promptly handed over to Lisa to play the machines.

'Not worth walking away with,' he said when she would have protested. 'Try that one over there.'

She did so, mesmerised by the woman at the next machine who had several racks of silver dollars and was feeding them in like an automaton while paying little heed to the pile already lying in her out tray. Gaining a ten-coin pay-out herself, Lisa had to acknowledge a certain buzz. There was always the feeling that one more go might be the one to set the big bell ringing for the twenty-thousand-dollar pay-off.

They took time out in Caesar's for a drink and a rest. Sipping her iced daiquiri, Lisa looked across at the man seated opposite and wished she could only read the mind behind the impenetrable grey eyes. Apart from putting a hand beneath her elbow when they dodged the teeming traffic to cross the road, he had made no attempt to touch her, but that didn't mean he had forgotten their altercation earlier that day. 'I'm going to take a great deal of pleasure in fetching you down off that soapbox', he had said. So far as she knew, this was simply the softening-up process.

'Enjoying it?' he asked.

'Yes,' she admitted reluctantly. 'Not that I'd want to spend more than a couple of days here.' She paused. 'You've been before?'

He shrugged. 'Once or twice. The only gambling I normally indulge in is on the stock market.'

With excellent results, Lisa was sure. She said levelly, 'This take-over was kept very quiet. Any particular reason?'

The shrug came again. 'Just the way we work.'

'We?'

'Brecket-Copeland, the parent company. The travel industry is only a part of our interests.'

'The part you're in charge of.'

'By choice. It's an ever-growing concern. We aim to control a major section of it. With so much competition around, reputation is vital. Hence the need to make sure we're giving value for money. I made spot choices out of the tours on offer with Leisure, and put someone on each. I took this one myself purely on a whim.' He paused there, eyeing her with lifted brow. 'Anything else you'd like to know?'

There was plenty, but she wasn't about to admit it. 'It just seems incongruous for someone in your position to be doing this,' she murmured.

'I already told you, I prefer first-hand experience. I'm not into sitting about an office all day. What about you? Don't you have family back home?'

Her throat tightened. 'No. Isn't it time we were making tracks back to the hotel? It must be nearly midnight.'

'The witching hour.' There was mockery in the comment. 'I guess we both of us had an earlier start than most. Are you going to finish your drink first?'

Lisa shook her head. 'I've had enough.'

He called over the pert and pretty, skimpily clad waitress and paid the bill, raising a genuine smile when he told her to keep the substantial change. People were still piling into the place when they left by the impressive front doors, stately limousines rolling up to discharge occupants in evening dress. The night was only just getting underway for most, Lisa gathered, but felt no wish to stay and partake. Enough was enough.

They walked back to their hotel in near silence. Still in the high seventies, the temperature was moderated by a hair-ruffling desert breeze. She would never forget this scene, Lisa told herself, viewing the sparkling length of street stretching ahead. She would never forget the man at her side either, but for very different reasons. He made her feel all churned up inside.

They found the Fullers in the lobby. June was missing, announced the girl's mother, looking drawn with worry. They had looked everywhere for her.

'We got separated in one of the casinos a couple of hours ago,' supplied the father.

'Where's Ben?' asked Lisa.

'In bed,' he said. For once even he appeared concerned. 'We were just going to set out and look for her again.'

About to offer to go with them, Lisa let the words die in her throat as the outer doors swung again to admit the very person in question. She was accompanied by

Dean. The latter's smile faded a little when he saw the reception committee.

'I ran across her right up by Circus Circus,' he said swiftly as Mrs Fuller gave a cry of relief. 'I guess she went the wrong way looking for you guys.'

June herself was under no immediately apparent strain. She'd spent ages trying to find them, she said in answer to parental reproof. How had she been supposed to know which direction their hotel lay in? She hadn't even been able to remember the name of it.

A master stroke, forestalling the obvious question, thought Lisa drily, with her suspicions well and truly cemented. Dean must be mad encouraging a sixteen-year-old girl!

'All's well that ends well,' commented Reece as the family trio made their way to the lifts. 'It could have been worse.' The glance he rested on Dean was narrowed. 'Lucky you happened to be in the vicinity, or she might have been wandering round all night.'

The younger man didn't turn a hair. 'Sure was.' Passing from Reece to Lisa and back again, his own glance held a sly speculation. 'You and Miss Bellman planning on doing the Hoover Dam trip tomorrow?'

'I shouldn't think so,' came the smooth reply. 'I already saw it.'

Lisa closed her mind to the sudden sharp pang of disappointment. Why should she have taken it for granted that he would be taking the side trip? He probably had better things to do right here in town.

They all travelled up in the lift together. Reece got out at the third floor with an expressionless and impersonal 'Goodnight,' leaving the two of them to continue to the fifth.

'Had a good evening?' asked Dean on a bland note.

'Better than June's parents,' Lisa replied meaning-fully. 'You had an arrangement with her, didn't you?'

The lift came to a stop again. Dean waited until the doors had opened and they were outside in the corridor before answering. He made no attempt to deny the allegation.

'The poor kid needed a break from that mother of hers.'

'You admit she's just a kid, then?'

His grin was reminiscent. 'In years, maybe. She's not exactly backward in coming forward.'

'Only with encouragement! Surely there's enough en-tertainment for you around here without taking on schoolgirls?'

'Hey, what's with the mother hen bit?' He was beginning to sound hostile. 'You take care of your brood and I'll take care of mine. The last thing I need is advice from a temp!'

'I'm not the one to watch out for,' she came back recklessly. 'As you say, I'm just here for this one tour.'

He caught her arm as she made to turn away to the door of her room. The good-looking features held a suddenly altered expression. 'What's that supposed to mean?' he demanded.

Already regretting the hasty retort, Lisa made an attempt to bluff her way out. 'June's father might have something to say if he catches the two of you together.'

'Are you threatening to tell him?'

She shook her head, thankful that he appeared to have accepted her stratagem. 'I've no intention of telling either of the Fullers anything. All I'm saying is you're running a serious risk.'

'My affair, not yours.' He let her go, giving vent to a sudden sigh as he ran an eye over her. 'You know, we could have been real good together.'

'Not in a million years,' she told him crisply. 'Goodnight.'

She was glad to be inside her room again with the door safely shut. Any obligation she might have felt towards putting Dean in the picture had vanished. He deserved whatever he got. Telling June's parents what their daughter was up to might be beyond her, but she could and would keep an eye on the girl from now on. Sixteen was too young to be playing around with a man ten years older, even if the latter could have been trusted not to take things too far.

The burr of the telephone took her unawares. She went over to lift the receiver with a fluttering sensation under her ribs.

'I want you,' announced Reece without preamble. There was a pause as he waited vainly for her to reply, a suggestion of a smile in his voice when he spoke again. 'Don't pretend you're surprised.'

Lisa found her voice by sheer effort of will. 'Is that why you got rid of Sandra?'

'Part of it. You could say she talked herself into an early departure.'

She couldn't quite eradicate the tremor. 'You're quite ruthless, aren't you?'

'If that's the way you see it.' He sounded amused. 'I don't believe in holding back. Life's too short. And before you say it, I'm aware that's a cliché.'

'I wasn't going to say it,' she denied. 'I...wasn't going to say anything.'

'Not even no?' The amusement was still there. 'I'll take heart from that.'

'Don't bother.' She was regaining some stability now, both emotionally *and* physically. 'Five days might be long enough for you, but I'm not out of the same mould as the women you're accustomed to dealing with.'

'I know.' This time the tone was softer. 'It's what drew me to you the very first day we met. An indefatigable spirit, it's called.'

Just a line, Lisa told herself, stifling any response. She should put down the receiver on him, but that wasn't enough. She had to convince him once and for all that there was no chance of her entering into any kind of liaison.

He forestalled her with a gentle 'Sleep well,' and rang off. Following suit, she scarcely knew whether to laugh or cry. The man had her going round in circles, too confused to know what day it was. Only he needn't imagine he was going to confuse her into bed with him. She was here to do a job, not provide light relief for a bored executive.

With more than half the tour members eager to see the famed Hoover Dam, it was necessary to take both coaches, to Dean's ill-concealed disgust. He was cool and sarcastic towards Lisa, who schooled herself not to show any reaction. With ten days still to go, this was no time to start a war.

The Fuller family were present in force. June looked mutinous when refused permission to ride on Dean's coach. There were more spare seats than occupied ones on his, she pointed out. It made sense to share the passengers evenly between them. Ben could come with her.

Ben scotched any hope she might have had by flatly refusing to make the exchange. He came up front to sit beside Lisa instead, on the pretext of asking her about the dam. Lisa didn't mind. It took her mind off other matters for a while.

Reece hadn't put in an appearance at breakfast. Tired after a restless night, she had been relieved not to have to face him. All very well to keep telling herself he wasn't worth a second thought, but that didn't oust his image from her mind's eye. If he kept up this attack on her senses, there was even the possibility that she might eventually succumb.

The dam itself was surrounded by a veritable sea of cable-carrying pylons stuck haphazardly into the bare brown rock. Lisa photographed the awe-inspiring swoop of the vast white face, but elected to wait up top in the sunshine while the rest of the party took the scheduled tour of the inner workings. She felt depressed enough without spending an hour underground.

This had to stop, she told herself desperately. Reece Harland was simply not worth losing any sleep over. His offer to help her stay on in the States couldn't be relied on, even if she had been prepared to pay the price. Ruthless, she had called him, and she saw no reason to go back on that assessment. His kind took advantage of any ruse to further their aim.

They got back to Vegas at four o'clock after a two-hour sojourn at the Lake Mead marina for swimming and boat trips. Ben Fuller was in his seventh heaven with twenty dollars in his pocket from a lucky win at the restaurant where they had eaten lunch. Being under age, he wasn't allowed to play the casino machines.

'I'm going to buy something special,' he declared when one of the American contingent asked him how he was going to invest his winnings. 'I haven't decided what yet.'

There was no sign of Reece in the lobby. Going to collect her key from the desk, Lisa was handed an envelope bearing her name in a decisive hand she couldn't fail to identify. The note inside was short and to the point. 'I'll be in my room from four. Call me when you get back.'

No way, she thought determinedly. From now on, she stayed as far away as possible from the man.

She was washing her hair when the telephone rang. Too well aware of who the caller might be, she attempted to ignore it, but it went right on ringing until she simply had to answer.

'I called the desk,' said Reece. 'You got my note.'

Lisa sat down on the bed edge, rubbing her hair with the towel. She kept her voice expressionless. 'That's right.'

'So I'm taking you out to dinner somewhere better than this,' he said. 'And that's an order, just in case you were thinking of refusing.'

'I'm off duty now,' she pointed out.

'You're still under company employment, and subject to orders from above.' He didn't give her time to reply. 'Seven o'clock in the lobby. I thought we'd do a show after we eat.'

She had three choices, Lisa reflected, sitting there with the receiver still in her hand. She could leave the hotel before seven and lose herself along the Strip, she could simply stand by her guns and refuse to accept his dictum, or she could . . . comply.

The first was out because Las Vegas was still no place to be on one's own, the second hardly more likely to succeed than it had last night, when it came right down to it. Which left her with little choice at all, she conceded, trying not to heed the deep-down part of her that had known all along what the decision would be. Only dinner and a show was as far as things were going to go. Any attempt to further last night's declaration, and that would be it!

Considering the American lack of formality on holiday, and the restricted nature of her wardrobe, she plumped for the simple white linen sheath dress, with a heavy gold necklet as her only jewellery apart from her wristwatch. Her hair was ready for trimming again, she thought critically, viewing her reflection in the mirror before leaving the room, but it would have to do until they got to Los Angeles.

Wearing a pale beige suit in an ultra-lightweight cloth that still managed to retain its superb styling, Reece was already waiting in the lobby when she got down. Looking at him, recalling what he had said on the phone last night, Lisa felt the familiar tension curling up from her toes, and was hard put to it to stop it from showing in her voice as she answered his greeting.

'I'm here under protest,' she added. 'I hope you realise that.'

He smiled and shrugged. 'Duly noted.'

He took her to the Dunes Ocean restaurant for the most superb seafood she had ever eaten. The lighting and décor were designed to give the impression of being under the sea. Seated in the centre of the room, the harpist was more celestial than oceanic, but who, thought Lisa, was complaining? Everything in Vegas was over the top.

She found herself loosening up as the evening progressed. Lacking the caustic edge for once, Reece himself was a different proposition. Telling him about her parents was surprisingly easy. He offered no sympathy, nor did she want any. There were ways of just listening that were far more meaningful.

One of America's top female vocalists was fronting the bill at Caesar's. The whole show was lavish, the chorus line-up equal to any the *Folies Bergère* could command. This tour had to be the most diverse she had ever experienced, Lisa acknowledged. From snow-capped mountains to desert wilderness to neon city, and not even halfway through.

Reece rolled some dice in the casino afterwards. At his instigation, Lisa had a go too, and was thrilled to win fifty dollars.

'Good thing we're leaving tomorrow,' she laughed as they moved on, 'or I might get the bug!'

'You won't find any casinos in Utah,' agreed Reece. 'It's strictly Mormon country.' He glanced at his watch. 'I guess we should call it a day.'

Now for the reckoning, she thought, feeling her heart jerk. He hadn't spent the whole evening entertaining her for purely altruistic reasons. Only he needn't think he was going to get her into bed on the strength of it either.

It was gone one o'clock when they reached their hotel. As she had anticipated, he made no attempt to stop the lift at the third floor, but continued with her to the fifth. Walking along the corridor, she was vibrantly aware of his lean strength—of the tumult of emotion building inside her. What she felt for this man was more than just attraction, she knew now, but how much more? And what difference did it make, anyway, when all he wanted from her was a purely physical gratification?

Reaching her door, he took the key from her nerveless hand and inserted it in the lock. Tongue frozen to the roof of her mouth, heartbeats like thunder in her ears, she preceded him into the room. She heard the door close again, and felt every nerve in her body quiver as he turned her towards him.

The grey eyes were narrowed, his mouth sensually curved. When he kissed her it was lightly at first, almost playfully, his lips teasing hers apart then withdrawing a little, making her follow him. The words of dismissal she should have used outside the door were still there in her mind, but no longer quite so vital. There was no harm in this, only pleasure. She couldn't find it in herself to cry stop.

The feel of his hand on her breast was excruciating. She knew a sudden surging need to be free of the encumbering clothing, to have that same hand exploring her whole body—to explore in her turn the vital, muscular lines. Making full, complete love with Reece could only be wonderful; he wouldn't allow it to be anything else. She ran her fingers up into the dark hair, loving the crisp, clean thickness. Too late to turn back now; she wanted what he wanted; everything he wanted.

It was Reece who did the stepping back. He wasn't, Lisa realised through a sudden mist, even breathing faster.

'Heavy day tomorrow,' he said. 'Best get some sleep. I'll see you at breakfast.'

He was gone before she could speak, leaving her standing there gazing stupidly at the closed door. He was just playing with her, came the thought, followed by a wave of misery so acute she wanted to die. How amused he must have been at the ease with which he had undermined her resistance. She was too much of a push-over even to bother with, apparently.

That latter notion was all the more soul-searing for its basis in fact. Six short days, that was all it had taken. How were the mighty fallen!

She gave breakfast a miss. Already waiting at the coach when she got there, Barry gave her an appraising glance.

'Gambling the night away, were you?'

'Only part of it,' Lisa returned, conjuring a smile and a light note. 'Don't you ever get tired of all this?'

He shrugged. 'It's a living. Better than sitting in an office all day. We switch routes every so often, so it's not that bad.'

Checking the ice supply, she said, 'Are you married?'

'Twice,' he acknowledged. 'Both failures.' He sounded philosophical about it. 'Main reason I took this job. Nothing much to stay home for. How about you? No boyfriend waiting back home?'

She didn't look up. 'If there were, I wouldn't be here.'

'Footloose, eh?' He paused. 'Caught a glimpse of you in Caesar's last night with the Harland guy. What happened to the blonde bombshell?'

'She was called home.' Lisa was glad to see the trickle of passengers beginning to emerge from the hotel. 'Better start getting the bags on board.'

Dean was late. Most of his people were already on board by the time he put in an appearance. The enmity was still there in his voice when he spoke to Lisa. If there was any way he could drop her in it, she thought, he would. Rejection such as she had doled out was not to be taken lightly.

They were doing a last check of the day's itinerary when Reece arrived. Lisa couldn't bring herself to meet the grey eyes, and the mockery she knew would be there. She could feel the tell-tale warmth in her cheeks, and fought to keep her voice steady. No one must be allowed to guess what she was feeling—and particularly not Reece. He'd exhausted what potential he had seen in her. Now, probably, he would leave her alone.

She had to face him eventually, of course. In the confines of the coach, and with duties to perform, there was

no other choice. Several people had asked him where
Miss Bellman had got to. She had returned home for
personal reasons, he had answered smoothly, and left
them to interpret that any way they liked. His expression,
when Lisa handed him a coffee, was difficult to read.
At least he wasn't taunting her with last night's ignom-
inious surrender.

They went north from Vegas, crossing into Arizona
for a brief period before hitting the Utah state line. Lunch
was taken at a tiny little place called Springdale just prior
to entering Zion National Park. With Dean still keeping
his distance, Lisa found herself sitting alone at the table
for two in the cabin diner. Having Reece take pity on
her was galling in the extreme.

'I'd as soon you didn't bother,' she said stiffly. 'I
actually prefer my own company.'

He lifted a well-schooled eyebrow. 'Is that a fact?'

'Just go away.' This time she was unable to keep the
slight tremor from her voice. 'You said everything you
had to say last night!'

'I was under the impression I'd left a whole lot that
needed to be said.' He studied her for a moment, a
curious expression in his eyes. 'You'd rather I'd stayed
on?'

'No!' The denial was too swift and too fierce; she made
an attempt to modify it. 'I'd rather you'd never been
there in the first place.'

'Because you suddenly found yourself indulging a
perfectly natural emotion?'

'Because I barely know you.' She was desperate to
escape this conversation. 'Just forget it. I shall.'

'I'd doubt that from the way you're acting.' He shook
his head in mock sorrow. 'There I was, consoling myself

I'd done the right thing for once. Some sacrifices just aren't appreciated, I guess.'

Lisa was silent for a long moment, gazing at him, still suspecting some ulterior motive. 'I'm not sure what you're supposed to be suggesting,' she said at last, 'but I'd as soon leave the whole subject alone.'

'I wouldn't.' The tone of his voice brooked no argument. 'You thought I'd walked out on you because I'd lost interest, is that it?'

She lifted slim shoulders, trying for a level note. 'Something like that.'

'If I'd left it another minute you'd have been in no doubt. I just didn't want to rush you into something you weren't quite ready for, that was all.'

They were far enough away from the other tables for the low-toned conversation not to be overheard, but they were attracting some speculative glances from those in the vicinity, Lisa realised. 'Are you always so forbearing?' she asked, and saw the strong mouth tilt.

'That's what they call a loaded question. Let's just say you're a different proposition from most.'

'Because I'm English?'

He laughed. 'That might have something to do with it. Anyway, do I take it we're friends again?'

'Friends' hardly covered the way she felt, Lisa admitted wryly. Reece was like no other man she had ever met. He had her spinning like a top. Today was Saturday. A week tomorrow they would be back in San Francisco. Between then and now lay eight whole evenings—to say nothing of the nights. There was no way she was going to get through that length of time keeping him at arm's length. No way she even wanted to, if she was honest about it.

'I guess so,' she said, adopting an American accent and drawing an appreciative grin. Looking across at the lean, tanned face, she felt her heart contract. The danger of losing it altogether was more than a possibility: at the moment, it was close to actuality. And *that* he certainly wouldn't want.

CHAPTER SEVEN

ZION was a magnificent showcase of rainbow-hued rock formations. Making for the east gate, after taking in the main sights, they had to be escorted through the Mount Carmel tunnel as single-lane traffic owing to their width of vehicle. Occasional windows cut through several feet of rock provided glimpses of awesome canyons and untrodden mountainside. Lisa wasn't sorry to be out in the sunshine again. The thought of all that weight pressing down on the roof of the tunnel had not been a comforting one.

Set high up above the southernmost point of winding, twisting Lake Powell, Page offered the most luxurious accommodation of the whole trip. Lisa's room was huge, and beautifully furnished, with sliding glass doors opening on to a terrace overlooking just one of the inlets of which the lake shore consisted. There was little, if any, vegetation to be seen, just mile after mile of red-gold rock.

No place to live if one liked trees, Lisa reflected, coming back indoors to start sorting out something to wear for the evening. The temperature out there was searing even at this hour.

More than half expecting some communication from Reece, she was still thrown into something of a panic when the knock came on her door around seven. Ready, apart from brushing her hair, she went to answer the summons, her light word of greeting fading from her lips on seeing who was standing there.

Dean's expression was set, his eyes like chips of blue ice. 'You knew, didn't you?' he accused. 'That's why you've been sucking up to the guy!'

It would have taken an idiot not to know what he was talking about—an even bigger one to try pretending. Lisa looked back at him steadily. 'I've been sucking up to no one, but we'll leave that aside for now. How did you find out?'

'I had a message waiting for me from a colleague.'

'The same one who tipped you off about the take-over?'

'Right.' He thrust past her into the room, taking her by surprise before she had chance to object. 'What I want to know is, how long *you've* known.'

'Since Yosemite,' Lisa acknowledged. 'Miss Bellman told me, if it's of any interest.'

'That why he got rid of her?'

'So far as I'm aware, she had to return home for personal reasons.' Lisa was doing her best to stay calm and collected. 'Will you please leave, Dean? I've still to finish getting ready.'

'To meet Harland—same way you've done this last couple of nights?' He ran a jaundiced eye over her trim figure in the beige silk jumpsuit she had elected to wear. 'There's no guarantee you'll get a green card out of it, if that's what you're hoping. Brecket-Copeland don't control Immigration.'

Lisa resisted her impulse to close the door as someone passing along the corridor outside glanced in curiously. 'I'm not after a green card,' she said flatly. 'Once this job is finished, I'll be moving on.'

'Sure.' He paused, then burst out savagely, 'You could have warned me!'

'Why?' she asked. 'So you could put on a show of reliability for once? If you were interested in doing the job properly, you wouldn't need any warning in the first place.'

'You self-righteous English bitch!' The good-looking face was tight with fury. 'Who the hell do you think you are?'

Lisa gripped the door handle a little more firmly. It wasn't in her nature to be deliberately nasty, but this scene had to be terminated now before it went too far.

'If you don't leave,' she said, 'I'm going to start yelling for help to put you out. That would hardly improve your image, would it?'

For a moment she thought he was going to defy her threat. Eyes glittering, he looked capable of inflicting bodily harm on her. He pulled himself together with an obvious effort.

'Don't imagine I'm going to forget this,' he gritted as he moved past her through the doorway. 'I'll pay you out!'

Alone again, Lisa drew in a long, steadying breath. Just talk, she told herself. There was little he could do to hurt her. It would be interesting to note his behaviour so far as his job went from now on though. At least the passengers might benefit from an increased concern for their welfare.

Reece joined her at dinner in the crowded restaurant. The hotel was full to bursting point, he said, with another touring party in addition to theirs.

'The Canyon is going to be extra busy this time of year too,' he added. 'It's only fifty miles or so down to Cameron from here, then another fifty along the east rim road. Allowing for stops, we should be at the village by mid-afternoon.'

Looking at the menu, Lisa said slowly, 'You must have made your assessment by now. Do you really need to see it through to the end?'

'Need, no.' His tone was light. 'I guess I'm entitled to take the rest as a vacation.'

'Hardly your usual choice, I'd have thought.'

'No?' He waited for her to glance up, lifting a quizzical eyebrow as she did so. 'And what, in your estimation, would be my choice?'

'Something active,' she said. 'Skiing, sailing, horse riding...'

'You could be right at that. Did you ever do any sailing yourself?'

'A little,' Lisa acknowledged.

'Then you'll have to come out with me when we get back to Frisco.'

'I'll probably be moving on after we get back.' It wasn't what she had meant to say, though eventually it had to be true. 'The girl I'm staying with only has a very small apartment. It isn't really big enough for the two of us on any long-term basis.'

'How long did Immigration give you in the country?'

'Three months. I'm due to leave on or before the thirty-first of August.'

'That's over eight weeks away still.'

She glanced at him briefly and away again, unable to sustain the penetration of the grey gaze. 'It depends on Jane's willingness to put up with me that long.'

'She might not have to.' His tone was easy, lacking any kind of undercurrent.

A young waitress paused at their table, order-pad poised and ready. Lisa said swiftly, 'Just the fillet, please. Medium rare. Baked potato with sour cream, and broccoli.'

'Same for me.' Reece waited until the girl had moved on to the next table before saying amusedly, 'You realise you ruined her spiel?'

Listening to the list being reeled off for the benefit of their next-door neighbours, Lisa could only smile and shrug. 'Not much point going through all that if you already know what you want.'

His eyes were on her mouth, his lips slanted. 'True. Do you fancy a stroll round the town before we turn in for the night?'

She could be saying yes to a great deal more than just a walk, Lisa realised, and suddenly didn't care. Once this next week was over, she might never see him again. And that was something she didn't want to contemplate.

The night was starlit and hot. Too hot to walk further than the brow of the hill. Despite its being a weekend, and comparatively early, the area was deserted, the shops closed, the only real sign of activity in the two battered cars full of teenagers drag-racing up and down the centre of the street.

With the nearest city of any decent size more than two hundred miles away, the residents of Page were almost as isolated as those in Death Valley, Lisa reflected. If this was Saturday night, what were the rest like?

'We're only just over the Arizona state line,' said Reece when she voiced the thought. 'The Mormon faith still holds sway. Emphasis is on education, sport and family life rather than evening entertainment. Those kids' parents would probably be horrified to know what they're up to right now.' He glanced down at her, expression enigmatic. 'Ready to go back?'

Lisa nodded. There was certainly nothing much to stay out here for. Her heart jerked as his arm settled lightly about her shoulders. The fingers curving her collar-bone were already possessive. If she was going to turn back at all, that time was now.

'I'm not sleeping with you,' she burst out before she could change her mind again, and saw his mouth twist.

'Ever heard of waiting till you're asked?'

Her flush went all the way through. 'I'm sorry,' she stumbled, 'I thought——'

'You think more than you listen, for sure.' It was difficult to tell from his voice what his mood might be. 'I'm not out for any one-night stand. I'd imagined I'd made that clear enough last night.'

Her own voice sounded husky. 'What *are* you out for?'

'Remains to be seen. As you so rightly pointed out, we barely know each other.' He stopped and turned her towards him, eyes reflecting the light from a nearby lamp. 'That's a matter I intend rectifying.'

His mouth was warm and compelling. Lisa responded instinctively, still not wholly certain that he meant what he appeared to be saying, but more than willing to be convinced. The attraction was mutual; she had known that almost from the first. Why not the rest?

'I'm . . . lost for words,' she murmured when he let her go.

He laughed drily. 'That's an achievement in itself. Let's get back.'

Apart from the duty receptionist, the hotel lobby was devoid of activity. They were on the same floor this time, Lisa paused with her hand on the knob, feeling the desire building inside her as she looked up at the man standing there. The urge to throw her cap over the moon and invite him into the room was so strong she could barely resist it.

Reece made no attempt to kiss her again. 'Have a good night,' he said, and went on his way, leaving her to open

the door with suddenly renewed doubt as to his serious-
ness. For all she knew, the whole thing might be his idea
of a joke. He could be laughing up his sleeve at her
gullibility.

In which case, he would surely have taken advantage
of 't, came the timely rejoinder. Was it possible to fall
in love in a week? she wondered mistily, and knew the
answer had to be yes. Reece Harland was everything she
could ever want in a man.

Commercialised though it undoubtedly was in parts, the
Grand Canyon proved no disappointment. Even though
Lisa had been prepared to a certain extent by countless
films and photographs, the sheer immensity of the great
rift overwhelmed her senses. Not just the size, but the
shapes and colours down there within the mile-deep, ten-
mile-wide chasm, all changing by the minute as the sun
lowered towards the western rim.

The waist-high stone wall edging the paved rim trail
seemed inadequate protection against such a drop. In
parts, there wasn't even that much. Seeing one passing
couple trailing two young children unattended in their
wake, Lisa could only hope the latter's guardian angels
were on the alert. She even followed the family for a
while, until a Ranger stopped them to point out the
danger they were running, much to her relief. She should
have had the guts to approach them herself, she reflected
wryly, but interference of that kind didn't come easily
without the authority to back it up.

She was on her way back to the hotel when she ran
into Dean outside one of the curio shops. The smile he
gave her was unexpectedly friendly.

'I've been looking for you,' he said. 'Want to forget
what I said last night?'

The blue eyes held no malicious backlight. Lisa shook off any misgivings to nod assent. 'It's forgotten.'

'Good.' He rested a hand on her shoulder, fingers caressing the bone. 'I don't want to fight with you, Lisa. It's the last thing I want.'

She had stiffened, yet couldn't bring herself to move too sharply away. 'It hardly makes for a good working relationship,' she agreed with delicate emphasis.

The hand fell back to his side, though the smile didn't falter. 'Not quite what I had in mind, but there's plenty of time.'

What exactly *had* he in mind? Lisa wondered, walking on. Hadn't she made it clear enough that there was nothing doing? Even without last night's nastiness, there had been no interest on her side. He had to be aware of it.

Mind occupied, she almost walked straight into a man coming in the opposite direction. The apology on her lips faded away as she looked up to meet Reece's enigmatic gaze. With one of the American couples insisting she join them for breakfast this morning, there had been no opportunity to talk together on their own since they had parted last night. Several times today she had wondered if she had read more than intended into what he had said. Feeling the way she did about him, it was all too easily done.

'You were quick off the mark,' he commented. 'I was anticipating a joint venture.'

'I wasn't sure what your plans were,' Lisa admitted. 'You'll have seen it all before, of course.'

'Only once, and that years ago.' His tone was dry. 'As you already guessed, I don't normally follow the tourist trail. Want to take another look, or did you have something else in mind?'

'Nothing pressing.' If asked, Lisa would have found it difficult to pin down the difference in him between last night and now, but a difference there was. 'Which way?'

'West,' he said decisively.

The pedestrian traffic thinned out considerably as they progressed along the Canyon edge. The shadows were lengthening, the colours becoming sharper as the sun's glare faded from white to gold. Dark cloud was drifting in from the north.

'Looks like a storm coming,' Lisa commented when they paused at an overlook to watch a couple of mountain goats leaping about a seemingly vertical face. 'I just saw lightning over there.'

Reece glanced her way. 'Scared of storms?'

'Not unduly—though I imagine one here would be pretty spectacular.' She hesitated before adding tentatively, 'Is anything wrong?'

The grey eyes turned her way again, the expression in them hard to define. 'Should there be?'

'I thought you seemed a bit . . . restrained, that's all.'

His smile was faint. 'Too many people around to be anything else. Had enough, have you?'

'Of the Canyon?' Lisa shook her head. 'I'm looking forward to spending the whole day here tomorrow. It's likely to be the only chance I ever get.'

'Once is all most people need.' His voice had lost that clipped edge. 'Your hair has a reddish tint in this light. Goes with the green eyes, I guess.'

The sudden mood swing lightened her heart. 'My mother was a redhead,' she said without the usual pang. 'She had the temperament to go with it too.'

'Like mother, like daughter.' He cast a glance at the steadily encroaching cloud cover as another lightning flash zig-zagged across. 'We'd better make tracks before that little lot gets any closer. Strikes aren't uncommon at this time of year.'

Lisa could agree with that. She'd been struck herself. Whether Reece felt quite the same degree of charge was still open to question, but the portents were good.

The storm wore itself out over the Canyon without coming any closer. Emerging from her room towards sunset, Lisa was startled to find Mrs Fuller right outside the door.

'We've lost Ben this time,' announced the latter, allowing the hand she had raised ready to knock to drop back to her side. 'He's been gone over two hours!'

'He probably lost track of time,' Lisa reassured. 'There's a lot to look at.'

'He was supposed to stay around the lodge until dinner,' said his mother, refusing to be soothed. 'We've been out to look for him, but there's no sign.'

Ben was fourteen, Lisa reminded herself, not four. He had enough sense to stay away from the edge.

'Did you contact the Ranger office?' she asked, and saw fresh alarm leap in the older woman's eyes.

'You don't think he's fallen over!'

'Not for a moment.' Lisa wished she could feel as certain as she sounded. All very well to tell herself it was unlikely, but there was no shortage of danger spots up here. Just a few weeks ago, she had heard someone saying, a man taking photographs out along the west rim had gone beyond the realms of caution and over-balanced. 'They'd be able to organise a proper search, that's all,' she added.

'Something wrong?' asked Reece. He had come along the corridor without either of them noticing him, standing now looking from one to the other in narrowed enquiry.

'Ben's missing,' supplied Lisa swiftly. 'There's every likelihood that he's simply wandering around, but——'

'We've looked everywhere,' the other woman broke in. 'Simply everywhere! We even went out as far as the museum. It's going to be dark soon.'

'Not for another half-hour.' Reece took charge effortlessly. 'Maybe he took the shuttle out along the west rim and didn't realise how long the round trip was. We'll go over to the terminal and ask it anyone's seen him, while you go to the Ranger office. He'll turn up.'

His air of calm authority seemed to offer some comfort to the woman. Only when they had parted from her outside, did Lisa voice any doubts.

'Do you really think he might have taken the shuttle?'

'Your guess is as good as mine,' he said. 'He's at the age where he's liable to slink off on his own just to get away from it all.'

Lisa cast an oblique glance at the lean profile. 'You sound as if you might be speaking from personal experience.'

He shrugged. 'Most boys go through that stage. This kind of vacation isn't geared to his needs. He should be with other kids his own age, not sitting around on a coach half the time. Some parents just can't let go.'

A shuttle tram was just coming in as they reached the barrier. Ben wasn't on it. The Ranger on duty shook his head when asked if he'd seen the boy.

'I only came on an hour ago though,' he said. 'This is the last shuttle in. We're closing down for the night now.'

The sun was almost touching the horizon. It was going to be fully dark within minutes of its setting, Lisa knew. Where else to look?

Reece moved to intercept the dozen or so alighting passengers. Most shook their heads in answer to his query. Only when he came to the final couple did he gain any useful response. They'd seen a young boy answering to that description out on Hopi Point earlier, said the man. They'd assumed he was with someone, naturally.

The Ranger was quick to act on the information. 'I'll go fetch a jeep,' he said. 'Hang on here.'

The sun had vanished by the time he returned with the vehicle, the lower depths of the Canyon merged into deepest purple. The missing boy hadn't turned up as yet, he advised, so there was every chance that he was still out there somewhere. The Fullers were being advised of the situation.

They passed plenty of people making their way back to the Centre on foot during the first mile or so of the drive, but after Maricopa Point, where the paved rim trail gave way to dirt track, the numbers dwindled to a mere trickle, giving out altogether from Hopi onwards. Apart from the engine sound, all was silent: a thick, weighty silence which seemed to rise from the depths and grab the throat. Only the lights beginning to wink from both south and north rims gave any indication that civilisation existed at all.

Reece had put Lisa in front next to the driver, and himself taken the rear seat. She could feel his presence like a rock at her back. Two weeks ago she hadn't even met him; now, she couldn't imagine life without him. If he meant what he said, she might not have to, only she couldn't fully convince herself as yet. It was all happening too fast.

They were more than two miles out when they finally ran down their quarry. Ben had left the trail to follow the curve of the narrow road. Hearing them coming, he stopped and waited, weariness in every line of his thin young body.

'I walked all the way to the Abyss,' he confessed when he was safely on board. 'I didn't know the shuttles were going to stop.' He hesitated. 'Is Mum mad?'

'Worried,' Reece supplied. His tone lacked any censure. 'What made you decide to take a shot at it tonight? There's all day tomorrow.'

'I wanted to do it on my own.' There was a hint of defiance in the set of the fair head. 'I never get to do anything on my own!'

There was nothing much one could say to that, Lisa considered wryly. His mother wasn't about to let go of the apron strings overnight. Her sympathetic smile drew a look amounting almost to worship. Not a lot she could do about that either, except try to discourage his sister and father from drawing attention to it. It was at least some distraction for the boy.

Both parents were waiting at the barrier. Retreated into stubborn silence, Ben was hoisted off by a father obviously intent on punishment. Watching them go, the Ranger shook his head.

'I've a boy that age myself. He'd as soon take a vacation with his folks as lie down and die! What that kid needs is some room.'

'I wonder what June's been up to while *she's* been on her own?' mused Lisa aloud as she and Reece moved towards the lodge. 'Not that she probably will have been on her own.'

'You mean Price?' The hard-boned profile looked austere. 'If he's up to any sort of game with that girl, his job's in the can. You can tell him that.'

'I thought,' she said, 'that you didn't want him to know who you were.'

They had reached the lodge entrance. He paused to give her a level appraisal. 'You're trying to tell me he doesn't already?'

Lisa could feel the tell-tale heat rising under her skin. 'Not from me.'

'Definitely from somebody. His whole attitude to the job changed overnight.'

'He had a message from someone at head office warning him,' she admitted, and was aware just how lame it sounded. 'I really didn't tell him myself,' she stressed.

His shrug was dismissive. 'It's not that important. Let's go and eat.'

Biting her lip, Lisa accompanied him outdoors. It was important to her that he believed what she said. Very important indeed.

Conversation over dinner was sparse. Reece seemed to have retreated into himself again. They were at the dessert stage before the Fullers turned up. Ben looked downcast, and scarcely spoke a word. Lisa's heart went out to him.

'Don't get involved,' warned Reece, catching her watching the family. 'You're likely to do more harm than good. Another week, and they'll be on their way home.'

He was right, Lisa knew. She had to stay out of it. 'Is your father still alive?' she asked.

'And kicking.' It was said without particular expression. 'He and my mother are separated.'

'But not divorced?'

'No. They find it impossible to live together, but they're neither of them prepared to take that final step.'

She would have liked to ask how he felt about it himself, but couldn't quite pluck up the nerve to delve that deep. He was so self-sufficient, it probably didn't matter to him either way.

One of the American couples collared her after dinner to ask her advice about various tours and visitor activities. Lisa refrained from pointing out that all such detail could be obtained from the free guide sheet, and did her best to work out some kind of itinerary for the following day.

'I guess you'll be spending your time with Mr Harland,' said the woman archly. 'A real shame his lady-friend got called back that way. You'd think he'd have gone with her, wouldn't you?'

'They weren't travelling as a pair,' Lisa said quickly, and wished she hadn't as she saw the woman's interest sharpen.

'I'd have sworn they were together!'

'What's it matter?' asked her husband with the long-suffering air of one too well-accustomed to such ferreting. 'I thought we were going for a drink?'

'Sure.' She patted Lisa's arm. 'Don't blame you for stepping in, honey. He's a real hunk!'

Reece was studying a noticeboard out in the lobby, hands thrust casually into the pockets of his trousers. Approaching him from the rear, Lisa could only agree with the woman's summing up. From the broad shoulder-line down to narrow waist and hip and firm male buttock, he was superbly built.

'Sorry about that,' she said a little huskily, joining him.

'All part of the job,' he returned. 'Would you like a drink?'

What she would really like, Lisa thought yearningly, was to be sure of what he was thinking and feeling at present. If he still doubted her word regarding Dean, she would rather he said so. Not that she had any way of proving her innocence, anyway. If he didn't believe her, he was hardly going to believe Dean.

She was no more certain of his inclinations when the time came to say goodnight. Longing for his lips on hers, she was left utterly despondent by his failure to even touch her.

'I'm taking one of the Canyon hikes tomorrow,' he announced. 'I need the exercise. It's a full day, so don't expect to see me before dinner.'

Lisa tried to keep her voice from reflecting her feelings. 'It sounds strenuous.'

'It is.' The smile was fleeting. 'I never could resist a challenge. What are you planning on doing with yourself?'

Pride gave her the control she needed to produce a careless shrug. 'As little as possible. Goodnight, Reece. Hope you enjoy your day.'

Just for a moment he seemed to hesitate, then he inclined his head. 'So do I.'

Closing the door behind her, Lisa stood for a moment grappling with the depression threatening to overtake her. This blow hot, blow cool attitude was hardly suggestive of any deep regard, was it? If he was simply amusing himself seeing how far he could lead her up the garden path, then it was time she put a stop to it. All it took was a little strength of mind.

CHAPTER EIGHT

THERE was no shortage of pastimes at and around the Canyon precincts. Lisa spent the morning in a combination of shuttle riding and walking along the west rim trail, ate a light lunch back at the lodge, then joined a fossil hunt for a couple of hours along with several other members of her own tour group.

Ben Fuller was there with his mother. The other two members of the family had elected to stay around the Centre, Mrs Fuller acknowledged when asked. She and Ben were the only ones interested in fossils.

Seeing the latter's listless expression as the guide discussed the various finds, Lisa wondered if he had been offered any choice in the matter. This whole holiday was turning out to be one long disaster from his point of view. Even if there had been others of his age group on the tour, it was doubtful if he would have been allowed any freedom. His mother was a clinging vine, likely to strangle every ounce of filial feeling before she was done.

There had been no sign of Dean all day. He might, Lisa supposed, have taken the bus down to Flagstaff or Williams rather than spend his free time mooching around here. Yesterday's overture had probably been made with alleviation of boredom in mind rather than any genuine desire to forgive and forget. With any luck, he wouldn't be repeating the exercise.

By six o'clock, with no word from Reece, she could stand the suspense no longer, and rang his room. The sound of his voice on the line brought relief, followed swiftly by mortification because he hadn't bothered to contact her. She was on the verge of replacing the receiver without speaking, but that went against the grain too.

'Had a good day?' she asked with forced brightness.

'An exhausting one,' he said. 'We only got back a few minutes ago.'

Hardly time to ring anyone, Lisa comforted herself. 'How far did you get?' she queried.

'Plateau Point. The longest twelve miles I ever covered!' There was a pause before he tagged on lightly. 'Fancy sharing a nice warm bath with me?'

Her laugh was equally light. 'I think you need it more than I do.'

'Too bad. Make it seven-thirty in the lobby, then. We'll eat down at the El Tovar for a change. OK?'

'OK.' It was all she could do to keep the elation within bounds. 'Seven-thirty it is.'

Ringing off, she wondered if and when he would have rung her had she not taken the initiative, then dismissed the thought as unproductive. She was seeing him. Let that be enough for now.

She dressed with particular care in an amber silk two-piece she hadn't worn before, and brushed her hair until it shone like silk itself. She had picked up some colour today, she noted, viewing her reflection in the dressing-mirror. It made her eyes look brilliant—or was that simply at the thought of seeing Reece again?

Tiring though the day must undoubtedly have been, he looked fit enough for another twelve miles when she did see him.

'Amazing what a half-hour soak will do,' he agreed when she commented on the fact. 'It wasn't so much the distance as the elevation change. Three thousand feet going down isn't so bad, coming up again at the end of the day is something else. Like mountain climbing the other way round.'

'At least you'll be able to rest tomorrow,' Lisa soothed. 'We've a two-hundred-mile ride to our overnight stop.' She added quickly, 'I rang through to the El Tovar and reserved a table in your name, by the way. Otherwise we might have been waiting hours.'

'Very efficient.' There was no sarcasm in the remark. 'You'd make the perfect secretary.'

She laughed. 'My typing is strictly the two-fingered variety, so that lets *that* out!'

'There's more to a good PA than an ability to type.'

They were outside by now in the delicious high-altitude coolness of the Arizona night. Lisa stole a swift, uncertain glance at him. 'You wouldn't be offering me a job, by any chance?'

His smile was enigmatic. 'Would you accept?'

'Only if it was all above board.'

'It would have to be. One thing we don't need is a run-in with Immigration.' He slanted a glance of his own. 'There are ways round the problem.'

She was willing to take his word for it. If Reece was prepared to go to that amount of trouble to keep her here in the States, she was more than prepared to go along. Her heart felt suddenly light as a feather.

She couldn't afterwards have said what they ate that night. Whatever it was, she scarcely even tasted it. Being in love brought a whole new perspective to life, she thought dreamily, watching the way Reece's mouth moved when he spoke—the strong line of his jaw. Nothing else seemed important any more.

The open collar of his casual blue shirt revealed a triangle of dark hair; she could feel her nipples peaking at the mere memory of how it felt to be held close against that broad hard chest, with nothing between them to mar the sensation. It was almost forty-eight hours since he had last kissed her. Right now, she felt she couldn't last out another ten minutes.

With the restaurant so crowded, service was slow. It was already approaching ten o'clock when they finally finished the meal. Primed by a particularly fine Californian Chardonnay, Lisa raised no objection when Reece suggested they call it a day. She wanted his love-making so badly she could hardly contain the need.

There was a moment outside her room when she thought he was going to leave her flat—a moment when his face looked suddenly stone-like in the dim corridor lighting—then he took the key from her nerveless fingers and inserted it in the door, following her in to lock it behind him again with a soft but meaningful click.

She went into his arms like a homing pigeon, too far gone to put up any pretence of reserve. Her kisses were feverish, her mind a tumult of emotion too long denied an outlet. No other man could make her feel this way, only Reece. Wonderful, masterful Reece! Whatever it took, she had to make him feel the same way about her.

He undressed her slowly but surely, kissing her while he did it. She quivered like an aspen leaf in a breeze when he bent his head to her bared breasts. His lips were gentle at first, so very, very gentle, increasing their demand by degrees until her whole body was on fire, her limbs trembling and unsupportive, her one desire to be with him as wholly and completely as it was possible to be. She said his name gaspingly, pleadingly, seeing the glitter in his eyes as he lifted his head at last to look at her.

'We have all night,' he said softly. 'Time enough for everything.'

The sheet felt cool beneath her back. Lying there, she watched him strip off his own clothing, breath catching in her throat at the sheer magnificence of him. He was so beautifully constructed, every muscle defined beneath skin tanned golden brown. A man who spent his leisure time outdoors, if not his working life; a man whom any woman with red blood in her veins would find irresistible. Even if she hadn't loved him, Lisa thought fervidly, she would still have wanted him.

She sobered a little when he came down beside her, aware of her inexperience and suddenly afraid of disappointing him. As if sensing some change in her, he lifted himself on an elbow to study her face in the moonlight flooding in through the window.

'What?' he asked softly.

'I'm not...what you're used to,' she got out. 'I don't...' She made a helpless little gesture, allowing the words to trail away.

'I'll be my own judge,' he said. 'Just be yourself.'

Still supporting himself on an elbow, he began a leisurely exploration of her whole body, fingers sensitised to every minute response. Lisa gave herself over completely to the sensation, feeling the melting heat flooding through her, the rising tide of emotion sweeping aside the last remnants of doubt. He knew so well where to touch, where to linger, how to tease with deliberate avoidance until she was almost frantic with desire.

His mouth was an endless source of pleasure. Gasping, mindless of everything but those seeking lips, she ran taut fingers through the thick dark hair, a part of her wanting to tear him away, another needing to hold him closer.

It was pure instinct that guided her to respond in kind, sliding her hands down over the smooth broad shoulders to seek the line of his spinal column and follow it down to the point where the firm flesh divided into twin hemispheres of tensed male buttock.

The lines of muscle about his waist followed through across his stomach, ridged like a washboard beneath her fingers. His hipbone was clearly defined. It was his turn to draw in a breath as she found him.

The movement came naturally, easily, eliciting a deep groan of pleasure and bringing a sudden sense of her own power. He took control again with an urgency she couldn't and didn't want to resist. She felt the full potent weight of him as he came over her, the surging thrust of his loins, then they were together—wonderfully, wholly together—and it was like nothing she had ever imagined, even in her wildest dreams.

How long it lasted she had no idea and didn't care. Time had no bearing on ecstasy. There was an inbuilt sensuality in her response to that driving, demanding force, moulding her limbs about him as if to keep him bound to her forever. They belonged to each other—two halves of one whole being. Nothing could part them now.

He remained where he was, holding her, after that tumultuous climax, dark head at rest on her shoulder. His skin was damp, the musky odour filling her nostrils a spur to emotions already rekindling. Lisa put her lips to his temple in a kiss that tasted of salt, and knew a moment of pure, unadulterated rapture that she was the source of his utter and obvious fulfillment.

'You,' he said gruffly, 'are one hell of a girl, Lisa Cunningham!' He eased his weight by rolling to one side, leaving a leg resting across both of hers. 'I feel as if I just went six rounds with Marciano!'

'No stamina,' she said, surprising herself with the teasing inflection.

His laugh came low. 'As I said, we have all night. Time enough for all things.'

Even for falling in love, she wanted to say, but couldn't quite manage the right note of flippancy. He would have to mention the word before she did—if things ever got that far. There was no certainty of it even now.

They made love again before they slept. Wakening at first light, Lisa lay for several minutes just watching the face on the pillow next to hers. To do this each morning would be bliss, she thought achingly, stilling the urge to reach out and run her fingers over the stubble-darkened jawline. Whatever happened, he would always be a part of her.

She was startled when he rolled over and reached for her, not having realised he was awake. His kiss set her instantly alight.

'What would you say to an early stroll along the rim to watch the sunrise?' he asked some time later. 'We're not leaving till eight-thirty.'

Lisa would have agreed to almost anything he cared to suggest right then. She felt at one with the whole world.

'Love it,' she said, and wished she only dare use the same word to him.

Early morning on the Canyon rim was chill. Lisa was thankful for the sweater and trousers she had donned in accordance with Reece's injunction.

He was dressed much the same himself, having returned to his own room for the purpose. Apart from one or two staff back at the lodge area, they appeared to be the first abroad.

The sun hoisted itself into view as they approached Grandeur Point, turning the sky to molten gold for a moment or two before the blue took over. It had rained again during the night, and the Canyon was filled with fog from rim to rim, eerie in its flat solidity.

As the sun climbed higher, the fog began to break up into separate clouds which lifted and vanished like will-o'-the-wisps, leaving the air so clear that every rock stood out in relief. Then, from the base of the cliffs, new mists began to rise as the moisture burned away under the warming rays, joining and becoming fog again before following the same pattern as before. The silence was tangible.

'It's primeval,' exclaimed Lisa in awe-struck tones. 'You'd swear no human would ever dare venture down there!'

'There are whole areas of it that have never been explored by man,' said Reece. 'Even the bit we covered yesterday is only accessible on foot or by mule, although somebody did drive a small bulldozer down as far as Indian Gardens a few years ago. Apparently they had a clearance of two inches either side of the path.'

Lisa's shudder was not put on. Just sitting here on one of the rocks edging the Canyon gave her palpitations. Without Reece she wouldn't even have ventured this far.

'Cold?' he asked.

About to shake her head, she desisted as he slid an arm about her shoulders. The sweater he was wearing felt smooth and warm to her cheek. Cashmere, at a guess. The kind of women he was accustomed to being with would take such things for granted—like Sandra Bellman, for instance.

'Why *did* Sandra go back?' she asked without really meaning to.

It was a moment before he answered. When he did it was expressionlessly. 'Does it matter?'

Another way of saying it was none of her business, Lisa concluded. Which was true enough, she supposed, although that didn't stop the rebuff from hurting.

'It's getting late,' she said. 'We ought to be making tracks. I still have to repack my case.'

Reece made no demur. Withdrawing the arm, he got to his feet. 'I need to do some sorting out myself.'

They weren't all that close to the edge, but it made little difference to her vertigo when she attempted to stand up. Seeing her face change colour, he caught her round the waist, holding her firmly until they were safely back on the path.

'You should have said how you felt,' he admonished, 'not just gone along with me. We could have watched the sunrise equally well from here.'

'But not as spectacularly.' She gave him a wan smile. 'I'm all right now, honestly.'

'You don't look it.' His expression altered as he studied her. For a moment he seemed on the verge of saying something else, then he apparently changed his mind, turning her in front of him along the narrow path. 'Let's get back.'

There were others up and about by now. They ran into several small groups making their way along to the Yavapai Museum to join the organised rim walk. None of their people were among them, Lisa was glad to note. With an eight-thirty scheduled start, they needed everyone together by eight-twenty at the latest.

Reece made no attempt to detain her when they reached the lodge. He seemed to have distanced himself again.

'See you later,' was all he said on parting, leaving her to consider a morning suddenly shorn of much of its brightness.

Dean came to join her at breakfast for the first time in four days. From his attitude, it would have been difficult to guess that anything untoward had ever taken place between them.

He'd spent yesterday down in Flagstaff where he had friends, he confirmed when Lisa asked. After three previous visits this year, the Canyon held little appeal.

'I'd have asked you along,' he said lightly, 'except that I guessed you might have other plans.'

'I did,' Lisa agreed. 'I can't imagine ever becoming bored with this place, no matter how often I saw it.'

He shrugged. 'Each to their own. I'm considering making this my last trip. This guy I met yesterday runs a modelling agency in LA. Says he can get me all the work I want.'

Over his shoulder, Lisa saw Reece come into the restaurant. His eyes rested on her for no more than a second or two before he turned away to follow the hostess.

'Sounds good,' she said tonelessly.

Dean glanced across at the man now taking his seat three tables away, coming back to Lisa with a certain calculation in the blue gaze. 'You feeling OK?'

From somewhere she dredged up a smile. 'Fine, why?'

'The way you looked just now.' He added blandly, 'This job's scheduled to get anybody down.'

'Only a few days ago you were saying it had its compensations,' she reminded him.

'Not enough. That Fuller kid won't leave me alone.'

'You shouldn't have encouraged her.' Lisa was too down herself to be anything but blunt about it. Finishing off her coffee, she put down her cup. 'Would you excuse me? Some things I still have to do.'

She forced herself to walk from the restaurant without so much as a glance in Reece's direction. Being virtually ignored by the man one had spent the night with was like being kicked in the teeth. Her attack of vertigo could hardly be responsible for the retreat, which left only one alternative. She had been right the first time. He had simply been playing her along. The game had been won with that phone call she had made. End of story.

She was in full control of herself by the time they began boarding. Enough so to face Reece without a flicker of expression when he came out with his bag. There was every chance he would be leaving them once they reached LA. He must by now have seen enough to make judgement on the tour's value for money.

He shook his head when she offered him coffee half an hour later, without looking up from the newspaper he was reading. Since Sandra's departure, he had had the use of both seats. Today, Lisa noted, there was a blue envelope file on the spare seat, as if laid aside after recent perusal. His notes on possible changes of itinerary, perhaps? There were one or two route changes she would make herself, if it came to that. Not that she was likely to be asked for an opinion.

Most of the day's driving was through desert country. Dotted along both sides of the freeway from time to time were Indian craft markets where it was possible to pick up hand-made jewellery and pottery for a few dollars. They stopped at a couple of the biggest by apparent prior arrangement—if the drivers' familiarity with the vendors was anything to go by.

A cut of the profits was an accepted perk of the job, Dean acknowledged when Lisa put the question. All the tour buses had their own scheduled stops.

'Don't try to tell me it doesn't happen in Europe,' he tagged on sceptically when she expressed her feelings on the subject. 'They're not losing out on the deal. That guy over there,' indicating one of the busiest stalls, 'runs around in a brand-new Cadillac. So who's doing the exploiting?'

It was an argument Lisa had been through before, and with as little chance of winning. Wisely she let well alone.

Turning to go back to the coach, she saw June Fuller staring at them from across one of the stalls where her mother was choosing beaded necklaces from around a dozen strung along her arm. The girl's pretty face wore an expression with which Lisa could only too readily identify. Unreciprocated love was devastating at whatever age it struck. At least Dean was no longer playing around, although the damage he had done already was more than enough.

They reached their overnight stopping-place just before three in a temperature touching a hundred and twenty degrees. Even Death Valley had been cooler than this, Lisa reflected, thankful for the icy blast from an air-conditioning unit turned up to full power.

The motel boasted a small pool set within a concrete enclosure. Heated by the sun, the water was too warm to be fully refreshing, but there were shaded tables around the patio and an iced drinks machine in a corner.

Still only halfway through her novel, Lisa did her best to focus her mind on the written word, with little success. Eventually she gave it up as a lost cause and sat gazing broodingly into the pool while she considered a grey-tinged future.

Tomorrow at this time they would be in LA, with three nights to get through before heading up the coast to Monterey and then back to base to complete the circle. Exactly what she was going to do when she did get back she still wasn't sure. Staying on in the States, even if she was allowed to, no longer held the same appeal. She'd been made a fool of by Reece, and it hurt. It was going to hurt for some time to come.

The scrape of the chair opposite being pulled out from the table jerked her out of her introspection. Reece sat down, resting an elbow on the shaded metal surface as their gazes clashed.

'There's something I need to get off my chest,' he said. 'Here's as good a place as any.'

'I was just about to go in,' Lisa responded stonily. 'There's really nothing to talk about, is there? You got what you were after. You don't need to worry that I might try making anything of it.'

The strong mouth took on a wry slant. 'I guess I asked for that. As I said yesterday, I never could resist a challenge, and you sure presented one.' He paused. 'You asked me this morning how I managed to get rid of Sandra. I did it by telling her the truth—that there wasn't a cat in hell's chance of getting it together. If I hadn't made the mistake of leaving the tour details on view, she wouldn't have been around in the first place.'

'And you might have achieved your aim even faster.' Lisa shook her head as he made to speak again. Her throat felt tight as a drum. 'I don't know why you're bothering to tell me all this, Reece. You had your fun, now let's both forget it!'

'I don't want to forget it.' His tone was steady. 'Last night was something special.'

Green eyes darkened. 'If you're hoping for a repeat tonight, you're out of luck. I don't give encores.'

'What I'm hoping for,' he said, 'is a fresh start. I originally planned on leaving the tour when we get to LA, but there's nothing so vital it can't wait until next week. Remember when I asked you to come and meet my mother? That took me by surprise too, at the time, but it's the best idea I ever had. The two of you have a lot in common. She doesn't pull any punches when it comes to saying what she thinks either.'

Lisa gazed at him with knitted brows, too over-whelmed by the sudden turn of events to think straight. 'I don't trust you,' she got out at last, and saw his lips twist again.

'I don't blame you. I've given you little enough reason. So it's going to be up to me to change that. Always pro-viding you want me to?'

She made a small helpless gesture. 'I . . . don't know.'

'So think about it.'

He stood up, bronzed shoulders blocking out the sun for a moment before he moved the few steps to dive into the pool. Lisa watched him with heart and mind totally at odds. He was making no false promises: a fresh start didn't have to mean a happy conclusion. All the same, he would hardly be going to that amount of trouble if he didn't believe they could form something worthwhile out of all this, would he?

CHAPTER NINE

THE wind came out of nowhere, picking up the paperback book Lisa had laid to rest on the table and swirling it into the air along with everything else not tied down. There were startled shouts from those still in the pool as towels and wraps lifted from their resting places, some flapping into the water, others finishing up flattened against the surrounding railings.

Grit stung unprotected skin and got between the teeth. Lisa felt a particle enter one eye, and clapped her hands over them both in protection.

Reece hoisted himself out of the pool without bothering with the steps, and came to take hold of her. 'Whirlwind!' he shouted in her ear. 'Let's get inside.'

Gathering their belongings as best they could, everyone had the same idea. The palm trees edging the lawns were whipping about in frenzy, the pool surface turned from calm blue to slopping, surging turmoil. Still covering her eyes, Lisa allowed herself to be guided by Reece across the car park and up the outside staircase to the balcony fronting the second-storey rooms. The relief when they were inside was marred only by the pain in her eye from the grit embedded there.

'Come into the bathroom,' he said. 'The light's better.'

Standing her in front of the small window, he opened up the eyelid with thumb and finger and used a corner of a clean flannel to extract the offending particle.

'There it is,' he said, showing it to her. 'Try splashing cold water into it now to rinse out any dust.'

The eye was watering enough as it was, but she obeyed the injunction, finishing off with a couple of mouthfuls to get the grit from between her teeth. Her hair was wet at the front when she lifted her head to the basin mirror. Reece handed her a towel.

'Does it often do that out here?' she asked. 'The wind, I mean. It was frightening! And so hot!'

'Straight off the desert,' he said. 'They're fairly frequent this time of year, but nothing to cause any concern. It's not likely to last more than fifteen or twenty minutes, although everything's going to be covered in sand when we go out again.'

Lisa slung the towel over the shower rail to dry off, self-conscious under his gaze. 'I don't think I'll bother. I wasn't planning on staying down there much longer, anyway.'

'So you said.' Reece moved away from the door to allow her access to the room beyond, following her through. 'It might be an idea to wait until it stops blowing before you venture out.'

It was only then, looking around at the scattered clothing and the tan leather suitcase open on the rack, that she realised it was his room they were in, not her own. The roomy shoulder-bag she used as a holdall was on a chair where he had dropped it on entering, her cotton wrap stuffed in the open top.

'I'm only just along the landing,' she said. 'I'm hardly going to come to any harm in a few yards.'

'So I'm asking you to stay.' His voice was soft, the hands sliding down over her shoulders and upper arms warm and firm and achingly familiar. 'Have you any idea what you do to me?'

Nothing compared to what you do to me, she thought mistily. She put up no resistance when he removed her bikini top, leaning back against him as he cupped her breasts in his palms. His wrists were so supple, the gold Rolex watch emphasising the sinewy strength. He hadn't taken it off in the pool, so it had to be waterproof, she found herself thinking irrelevantly, arching her back to the caressing movement of the long and tensile fingers. Only the best would satisfy Reece Harland.

'You're enough to drive a man to drink,' he murmured, lips nuzzling the side of her neck just below her ear.

Eyes closed, her whole body on fire, she could find no will to retreat from what was surely to follow. Whether Reece loved her or not was academic at the moment. What mattered was being together like this—wanting him the way she did. She met his lips hungrily when he turned her towards him. Arms about his neck, breasts pressed against his naked chest, she was lost to everything but the emotions rioting through her.

One hand entwined in her hair, Reece ran the other down her back to mould her to him by every intimate outline, kissing her with a devouring intensity that drew a like response. She moved her hips in reflexive sensuality against him and felt the answering surge. Desire was an aching need in every part of her body—a craving that could only be assuaged the one way and by this one man. She wanted him inside her, possessing her, driving out doubt as only he could.

There was little in the way of clothing left to remove for either of them. Lisa felt the air-conditioning playing over her for a moment or two as he lifted her on to the bed, then he was coming down over her, warm and hard and wonderful, kissing her temple, her eyes, and down the softness of her cheek to find her mouth at last in scorching demand.

Back arching, she opened to him like a flower, a moan of sheer pleasure torn from deep inside her throat at the incredible sensation as he took her to him. Making love with Reece was heaven—to lose him would be hell. But she wasn't going to lose him. Not now. He was going to love her the way she loved him, and forever!

All was quiet again outside when she finally and reluctantly roused herself from the delicious lethargy subsequent to total gratification. Reece lifted a hand and rested it on her breast, using the ball of his thumb to caress the tender flesh.

'There's no rush,' he murmured. 'We can stay here like this all night if we've a mind.'

On a purely practical level, that might be difficult, Lisa reflected, though she condoned the idea.

'I can't think straight when I'm with you like this,' she said huskily.

'About what?' He had followed the hand with his mouth, creating havoc inside her again with the lightly trailing touch of his tongue. 'Why not just go along with the mainstream and see where it leads?'

Because I'm too much in love with you to stand the uncertainty, she wanted to say, only it was too soon for that kind of declaration. Reece might want her, but that was still a long way from loving. She had to do as he said and just let things happen. At the very least, she could be with him.

He rolled suddenly on to his back, taking her with him and holding her there on top of him while he continued to kiss her. The tumult overtook her again, driving out all rational thought and leaving only sensation.

Six o'clock had come and gone by the time she finally reached her own room. Standing under the shower, she was aware of the deep and pleasurable ache throughout her whole body, of a swelling contentment. She might even have a bruise or two by tomorrow, but she didn't care. Life was nothing without this.

Tonight she would be with Reece again. There was no way she could stay away from him now. Keeping her feelings for him hidden from everyone else was going to be the most difficult part. To be on the coach with him tomorrow yet unable to touch him would kill her.

At least they had Los Angeles to come, she comforted herself, although meeting his mother would be the real testing time. Come Sunday, they would be back in San Francisco and facing the question of their future together. If marriage wasn't on the agenda then she would settle for whatever was. She would settle for just about anything rather than be parted from the man who had come to mean so much to her.

Smog lay like a pall over the whole of the Los Angeles basin, the cover seemingly so thick when viewed from the hills that Lisa anticipated grey skies and a gloomy atmosphere when they eventually dropped through it to reach the city below, and was both surprised and relieved to find she was wrong.

The eastern, industrial side of LA held little appeal for the sightseer. Sunset Boulevard itself, when reached, proved something of a disappointment in its long and dusty commercialised reaches. Running right through to the Pacific coast, it would no doubt alter out of all recognition when it reached the Beverly Hills area, Lisa concluded.

Tomorrow, they were due to take a morning tour of the main city sights, which would include Beverly Hills. Reece had already said he wouldn't be joining them, which was understandable, she supposed. What he had planned for the afternoon when she was free she wasn't sure. Providing they spent it together, she didn't really care.

The motel where they were scheduled to stay the three nights was close to the junction of Sunset and La Brea. Smallest so far of those they had sampled, it still boasted a fair-sized car park along with the usual pool and patio. American clientele demanded as much of even the cheapest places, Lisa had gathered over the course of the previous week and a half. Small wonder that they tended to regard Britain as still a mite primitive when it came to standard accommodation. The idea of sharing a bathroom with a whole floor was totally outside their experience.

Dean had been allocated the room next to hers again. It made sense, Lisa supposed, to place both couriers together, although few of the other places had bothered. Reece wasn't even on the same floor this time, which didn't exactly help.

He rang through some short time later to say they would be dining out. Telling her, not asking, Lisa noted, yet could conjure no resentment. He was accustomed to ruling the roost in his relationships, there was no doubt of that, but there would be time enough to sort out that aspect if and when some decision of importance to her cropped up. To demur just for the sake of it would be nonsensical.

She was showered and already dressed in a lilac and white cotton print when the half-anticipated knock came on the communicating door. Dean was wearing the same white trousers and black shirt he had worn that very first night back at Tahoe, this time with the addition of a linen jacket in a fine black and white stripe. Once again

Lisa found time to wonder at her total lack of response to his blond appeal.

'Thought you might fancy a meal out,' he said. 'This place isn't likely to run to anything special.'

'Nice of you to think of it,' she returned without regret, 'but I already made other plans.'

There was an expression in the blue eyes that was somehow disturbing. 'With Harland?'

'Well, yes, as a matter of fact.' She heard the faintly defensive note in her voice and took steps to eradicate it. 'With Reece.'

'You realise he's only filling in time with you,' he said. 'There'll be no follow-up once we're back in Frisco.'

'I'm not expecting any,' Lisa lied. 'Not that it has anything to do with you, in any case.'

His smile was tight. 'Just don't like to see you being taken for a ride, that's all.'

'So, close your eyes,' she retorted brusquely, and shut the door in his face.

That had been unnecessary, she acknowledged ruefully the moment she had done it. Allowing Dean to get to her was not only stupid but unfair on Reece. If she loved him she had to trust him—the two were surely synonymous? He would hardly be changing his plans to leave the tour here in LA if her body were all he was interested in, would he?

They met by arrangement down near Reception. Dressed in fine grey cords and toning, open-necked shirt, he set her heart thudding the moment she saw him. The expression in his eyes as he looked her over in turn was of slow reminiscence, causing her cheeks to warm a little as his gaze lifted again to her face. He knew what she looked like without any clothes at all—every intimate inch. Strange that she could be so totally uninhibited in lovemaking yet still be capable of blushing at the memory.

'I got Reception to call me a cab,' he said. 'We'll go and wait out on the sidewalk and save him having to manoeuvre round in here. I like the dress, by the way. Lilac's my mother's favourite colour.'

Lisa said lightly, 'I'll have to make sure to wear it when you take me to see her, then.'

'That's here and now,' came the level reply. 'We're expected.'

It took her a moment to steady her nerves enough to say, 'For dinner?'

Amusement gleamed momentarily in the grey eyes. 'Don't worry, she won't eat you. It will just be the three of us. Wednesday's her at-home evening. She's looking forward to meeting you.'

Lisa wished she could say the same. Her role in Reece's life was still too tenuous to make for confidence.

The yellow cab pulled in a moment later. Reece gave the driver the address, and followed Lisa into the back. Dusk was already creeping over the city, the lights springing to life. The pavements were all but empty of pedestrian traffic. Few people, it appeared, walked the city streets at night.

The Harland homestead lay up in the hills above Hollywood Bowl. Set within its own grounds behind tall iron gates, the house was old colonial in style and impressive in size. Viewing it as Reece paid off the cab driver, Lisa was aware of a certain sinking feeling at the base of her stomach. Property prices up here had to run into the millions rather than the thousands. She had realised, of course, that he was no bootstrap puller, but this kind of background went far beyond her speculation.

'Something wrong?' Reece asked as they mounted the broad flight of stone steps to the imposing iron-studded door.

'I just didn't expect all this,' she admitted. 'It's a bit overwhelming.'

'Too big for one person, I agree,' he said. 'It's becoming increasingly difficult to find staff, for one thing. Mother's reluctant to give it up, but she'll eventually have to. A service apartment would be ideal for her, if she could only see it.'

'Perhaps she can't stand the thought of being confined to one or two rooms after so much space,' Lisa commented, and drew an amused glanced.

'I wasn't thinking in terms of a *small* apartment. She'd need two rooms just for her wardrobe!' He paused on the top step to eye her consideringly. 'If you're thinking what I think you are, forget it. So far as my mother will be concerned, she'll either take to you or she won't.'

'And if she doesn't?' The question was forced from her.

One hand came out to tap her gently on the cheek. 'Just be yourself.'

She would have felt better if he'd taken her in his arms and kissed her, but he was already ringing the bell. The door was opened by an elderly man dressed conservatively in dark grey jacket and trousers. He greeted Reece with obvious pleasure and the familiarity of long acquaintance. Mrs Harland, he said, was waiting for them in the library.

Walking across the vast hall with her heels sinking into what felt like six inches of carpet, Lisa decided it was time to stop worrying about what kind of impression she was going to make. Reece was the only one whose opinion mattered to her, anyway.

Opening one of a pair of double doors towards the rear of the hall, he ushered her through ahead of him. Lisa had an impression of dark wood furnishings and tall curtained windows, but the focus of her attention was on the woman rising from her seat on a brocade sofa to greet them. Tall, and dark-haired like her son, and superbly clad in pale green silk, she had the face and figure of a thirty-year-old. Only in close-up was it possible to see the fine lines at the corners of her eyes and mouth.

'And not before time,' she said, without sounding too serious about it. 'It must be three months since you last came down.'

'Two,' Reece corrected. 'I was here for your birthday, remember?' He added easily, 'Meet Lisa Cunningham, from England.'

Lisa smiled at the older woman. 'Hello.'

The other's regard was openly appraising. 'Hello to you, too. Why don't you get us all a drink, Reece? Dinner won't be for another half-hour. I thought we'd use the breakfast-room, seeing it's just the three of us. The dining-room's too baronial.'

'I've been telling you that for years,' he said, moving to follow her suggestion while she invited Lisa to take a seat on the matching sofa opposite her own. 'The whole place is baronial. You'd be far more comfortable in an apartment—or even a hotel suite.'

'And what would I do with Grant?' she asked. 'He's been with us for too many years to just let him go.'

'He must be close to retiring age. Why not pension him off? The rest of the staff wouldn't have any difficulty finding other jobs.'

'I'll think about it.' She turned her attention back to Lisa, her eyes shrewder than her easy manner suggested.

'I understand this is your first time in America. Do you plan on staying?'

Lisa smiled and lifted her shoulders. 'I'd like to stay on, yes, but it isn't that simple. This job is purely temporary.'

Dark brows lifted. 'Job?'

'She's hostessing the Golden West Tour for Leisure Tours,' said Reece, bringing across three glasses on a silver tray. 'I took it you'd like your usual G and T,' he added to Lisa. 'More tonic than gin.'

'How come?' insisted Mrs Harland as Lisa took the indicated glass.

'One of the regular couriers was taken ill and they needed an urgent replacement,' Lisa explained. 'Once we get back to San Francisco I'll be back to square one.'

'I see.' Her glance switched momentarily to her son's face as he took a seat at Lisa's side, her expression not too difficult to define. 'So you're going to need help.'

'We didn't sort out all the angles as yet,' put in Reece on a casual note. 'There are ways and means.'

'I don't doubt.' Her own tone was dry. 'There are ways of running a company too. Having the vice-president of the travel division taking off on one of his own tours wouldn't be regarded as orthodox.'

His smile was unperturbed. 'How am I expected to know what a package tour is about without having experienced one for myself? I don't work to any rule book.'

'Like your father before you.' There was a certain underlying wistfulness in that statement. 'I should know better by now than to question anything you either of you do. At least there'll be continuity of a kind when you eventually take over from him.'

'Which won't be for another five years, if then. It will still be a board decision.'

Listening to the pair of them, Lisa was only just beginning to realise how far up the hierarchy Reece must actually be. The next step up from divisional vice-president could only be to group president, which meant that was where his father was now. It somehow put a different complexion on things.

Dinner was a beautifully prepared and served three courses of relatively simple fare. Lisa took a little of everything offered and tasted none of it. She felt out of her depth in this house, already judged an opportunist by the woman who lived in it, if she wasn't mistaken. Where Reece himself was concerned, she felt totally mixed up. Bringing her here to meet his mother at all seemed to indicate a more than passing interest, it was true, but that didn't have to mean any serious commitment.

They left at ten-thirty in a cab called out for them. Mrs Harland made no comment concerning her son's return to tour facilities, but Lisa could sense the dis-approval. She was quiet in the cab, gazing out on the glittering spread of the city below with eyes that regis-tered very little of the scene. With this kind of back-ground, Reece was never likely to know uncertainty about anything.

'Something wrong?' he asked as they joined the freeway heading downtown again. 'You've barely said a word since we left the house.'

'I didn't realise just who and what you are,' she said.

'So?'

'So you could have told me.'

'Why?' He said it quite calmly. 'What difference does it make?'

'Plenty. You saw how your mother reacted. She thinks I'm using you.'

'And are you?'

Her head jerked upright. 'Don't be ridiculous!'

The cabby showed no interest in the exchange, but Reece desisted from continuing it. Lisa could feel the warmth and pressure of his thigh through the thin cotton of her skirt, and wanted desperately to be in his arms. Only not until they had things straight between them this time. She was past all pretence.

She waited until they were back at the motel with the cab pulling away again before saying tentatively, 'I'd have thought you might want to spend the night at home rather than here.'

'It isn't my home,' Reece replied levelly. 'Hasn't been for years. In any case, I'd rather be here with you.'

She looked at him then, a long and searching look that gleaned little. 'Why?' she demanded at length, taking the bit firmly between her teeth.

His smile held a gentle mockery. 'I'd have thought that was pretty obvious. I can't stay away from you.'

Drawing in a steadying breath, she said, 'So what happens when we get back to San Francisco?'

'That,' he said, 'is something we have to talk about when we do get back. For the present, let's just concentrate on being together.' One lean brown hand came out to smooth a tendril of hair from her forehead, his touch setting her alight the way it always did. Eyes and voice were soft. 'Your room or mine?'

'I don't care,' she admitted, and meant it. Her own voice tremored with barely suppressed emotion. 'So long as *you're* not just using *me*, Reece.'

'If there was ever a time, it's past and gone,' he returned without hesitation. 'I'm looking for a whole lot more than a passing affair with you.' He drew her to him and kissed her with a passion that brought instant and consuming response, oblivious to any possible onlookers. 'A whole lot more,' he repeated gruffly when he came up at last for breath.

It was enough to be going on with, Lisa thought mistily as they made their way indoors. The rest could wait.

CHAPTER TEN

TOURING a city the size of Los Angeles, even when only taking in the main sights, was a lengthy and tiring process. Lisa was both surprised and delighted when Reece elected to join them.

It was difficult to equate the man sitting there so calm and possessed in his usual seat with the passionate lover of the night before. Lisa took care to avoid catching his eye too often, afraid of giving herself away to those seated near by. Most were aware of some rapport between the two of them, true, but hopefully not the extent. She hadn't acquired the kind of modern-day blasé attitude towards pre-marital sex that most of her age group could claim.

First stop was Hollywood Bowl. Set within a natural amphitheatre of hills, with tiers of seats rising to dizzying heights, the whole affair was both bigger and better than Lisa had visualised. There was a rehearsal underway for that evening's orchestral performance. Listening in, it was easy to imagine the same scene and sounds under starlit skies.

'I can get tickets if you'd fancy coming,' said Reece, strolling casually at Lisa's side as they returned to the coaches.

'I'd love it,' she responded eagerly, and drew a slanted smile.

'Then you shall certainly have it. I thought we might take a run out to a beach this afternoon—unless you've some other suggestion?'

She was far too happy to consider alternatives. 'Whatever you like.'

'What I'd like,' he said softly, 'is to spend the afternoon making love to you, but I guess that's being a mite too greedy.'

No, it isn't, Lisa wanted to answer, but Dean had swung into too close proximity for comfort. She made a point of moving away from Reece's side as they came up with the main body of their party. There would be time enough this afternoon and evening to be together.

The wide, tree-lined streets and luxurious dwellings of Beverly Hills had most people glued to their respective windows. Barry had acquired one of the maps purporting to show the locations of stars' homes. Lisa had her reservations about the authenticity, though she wouldn't have dreamed of ruining any illusions by casting doubts. People believed what they wanted to believe. It did no harm.

There was a call halfway through the tour at a huge open-air market. Turning away from the stall where she had bought an intricately worked cotton lace blouse as a present for Jane, Lisa bumped into the Fuller family. June gave her a glowering look that spoke volumes for her thoughts. Dean's defection was to be laid entirely at her door, Lisa gathered.

So long as he *had* defected, she didn't mind shouldering the blame. It would be best all round if he took that modelling job he had spoken of, she thought. That kind of environment wasn't likely to bring him into contact with vulnerable young girls.

Ben looked anything but happy himself. His mother supplied the reason.

'He wants to go on the Universal Studios tour tomorrow, but John and I don't care for that kind of thing, so we're not wasting money on taking the whole family.'

'I could go on my own,' muttered her son, drawing a laugh and a shake of the head.

'In Los Angeles? Of course you couldn't!'

'He could keep me company,' offered Lisa impulsively. 'I've been looking forward to seeing how a studio is run, but it's always better with someone else to talk to. We only have sixteen people down for the tour, so we'll just be taking the one coach.'

'I shouldn't have thought you'd be short of company,' put in John Fuller on a bland note. 'That Harland chap seems keen enough to supply it.'

'He isn't going.' Lisa addressed herself directly to Ben. 'I'd be glad to have you along.'

The flush was barely perceptible. Ben was, it seemed, learning to cope with his emotions. 'Great,' he mumbled.

His mother still looked doubtful. Short of suggesting that Lisa might be incapable of looking after a fourteen-year-old boy, however, she had little recourse but to go along. 'If you're sure,' she said.

Ben's grin was reward enough. He would at least have *some* happy memories of this trip to take home with him next week.

Reece had stayed at the coach park. He was chatting amiably with both drivers when Lisa returned there. Some of the passengers had beaten her to it, others came trickling back as the deadline approached. Dean was among the last, and he wasn't alone. Watching him take his leave of the two nubile blondes dressed in scanty shorts and even scantier tops, Lisa could appreciate their obvious mesmerisation. Even in uniform, Dean had star quality. He really was wasting his time doing this job.

Meeting Reece's eyes as she turned away to mount the coach steps, she gave him a swift smile, and was disturbed by his lack of response. Joining the tour had been a definite mistake on his part. It could be nothing but boring for someone born and bred in these parts. She would have to make up for it this afternoon when they were alone. The very thought of spending several hours doing exactly as they liked was wonderful.

Mann's Chinese Theatre was their last port of call. Photographing the famous and, in many cases, long dead names scrawled into the concrete, Lisa could only wonder at the small size of the hands and feet belonging to some past female stars. A size five shoe herself, she could fit little more than half a foot into Joan Crawford's imprint.

'Bet she didn't suffer from bunions!' commented one overweight spectator feelingly, easing her own protruding lump by taking off her shoe and rubbing the offending portion.

Laughing with her, Lisa felt a hand slide along her shoulder in a caressing motion too intimate to be anyone else but Reece's. Not that it was like him to be demonstrative in public. She looked round to make some light comment, the words fading on her lips when she saw Dean standing there. He was smiling, blue eyes glinting with a peculiar light.

'We're waiting for you, honey,' he said.

The woman with the bunion gave an exaggerated sigh. 'Wish I had somebody like you waiting for me!'

Lisa resisted the impulse to shake off the possessive hand. What kind of game Dean was playing, she wasn't sure, but here and now wasn't the time to make an issue of it. Having run around the block a couple of times, both coaches were now illegally parked for the pick-up a short distance down the street. She could see Barry gesticulating urgently from the driver's seat.

'We're liable to a hefty fine if we're caught in this zone,' he said as she climbed aboard.

'Sorry,' Lisa proffered. 'I got carried away.'

Reece was looking out of his window. He continued to do so during the rest of the comparatively short journey back to base. With the rest of the day free for individual pursuits, everyone dispersed when they got off the coaches. Lisa waited for Reece to make some approach, but he went off with the rest as if no arrangement had been suggested, leaving her to wonder if she could possibly have mistaken his intention. Not that it seemed likely when he already knew that tomorrow afternoon would be taken up with the Universal tour.

She waited in her room for half an hour before finally nerving herself to pick up the telephone. Reece took his time answering.

'I was in the shower,' he said when she made some light remark about being on the verge of ringing off. 'Right now I'm dripping all over the rug.'

Lisa took the hint along with the initiative. 'You said something about finding a beach this afternoon. Is it still on?'

'I guess so.' He sounded somewhat lacking in enthusiasm, but telephones were not the best conveyors of mood, Lisa reminded herself. 'I'll need to rent a car to get us there. Might be an idea if we had lunch first. Meet me in the lobby in twenty minutes.'

Definitely not the same Reece who had left here in the early hours of the morning, she thought disconsolately, replacing the receiver in its rest. She was only just beginning to realise how little she really knew him.

She put on a sleeveless white cotton jumpsuit for coolness and smartness combined, and wore a bikini under it. Reece was already waiting when she went down. Wearing cream trousers and deeper toned shirt, he looked fit for anything himself. He greeted her easily enough, but there was a certain restraint at the back of it, Lisa thought. If it lasted she would have to be blunt and ask him why. She could think of nothing she had either said or done that might have displeased him.

He seemed to relax over lunch. By the time they boarded a cab to take them to the depot where they would pick up a car for the afternoon, they were back on level footing again—on the surface at least. Sliding into the luxurious walnut and leather confines of the Trans-Am coupé, Lisa had to acknowledge that life at this level held a lot of attraction. Money might not be everything, but it surely helped!

The drive west along Sunset Boulevard covered some of the same ground they had covered that morning. Once past the huge pink sprawl of the Beverly Hills Hotel, however, they were in new territory. Reece drove with the confidence of one who knew exactly where he was going. Watching his hands on the wheel, so well in control, made Lisa tremor internally at the memories aroused. Two more nights here in LA, then one at Monterey, and they would be back in San Francisco. She looked forward to that eventuality with mixed emotions because she was still uncertain of his intentions. Marriage wasn't the be-all and end-all of a relationship, but could she really settle for anything less when it came right down to it?

It was further to the Pacific coast than she had anticipated. They turned south at Santa Monica, and finished up on a beach fringed by cultivated palms and already well patronised. Bronzed lifeguards seated on high in umpire's chairs kept a weather eye on the bathers.

Like herself, Reece had swimwear on under his clothing. They had neither of them brought towels, so would have to time their final swim in order to dry off before dressing again. The water itself was pleasantly warm, the waves not big enough for surfing though capable of sweeping her feet from under her, Lisa found to her cost as she came up spluttering from a premature immersion.

Reece was the stronger swimmer of the two of them, but he paced himself alongside her. Flying droplets of water glinted in the sunlight with every lift of a muscular arm.

'Had enough?' he asked when she paused for a moment to tread water and take in the heat-hazed inland scene.

She shook her head, very much aware of his near nudity in the brief black trunks, and of the answering quiver in her thighs. With his hair sleeked back, and strong bone-structure highlighted by the sun striking reflection from the water, he looked almost Latin.

'Look at me like that,' he warned softly, 'and I'm liable to try attempting the impossible!'

He reached out a hand and drew her closer, keeping them both upright by leg power alone as he kissed her long and hard on the lips. She could feel his arousal—the potent power in his loins. This way he left her in no doubt of how he felt. She kissed him back with honesty, making no secret of her emotions when she looked him in the eye again.

'I love you,' she said. 'I'm not sure if it's what you want, but it's how I feel.'

Apart from the sudden tensing of jaw muscles there was little discernible reaction. 'You hardly know me,' he said. 'This time last week, you were still standing me off.'

'Only because I dared not let you near me for fear of what it might lead to.' Lisa wound her arms about his neck, relying on his leg movements to keep the two of them from going under. His lips tasted salty. She used the tip of her tongue to lick the corner of the strong mouth, and felt his response in the shudder that ran though his whole frame. 'I never knew what being in love was like until now,' she whispered, losing all restraint in the overwhelming need to convey her feelings to him. 'I can't stop it from happening.'

'Why try?' His voice had thickened. 'Let's get back to the beach where we can talk in comfort.'

He kept pace with her as before. Emerging from the water to feel terra firma beneath her feet again, Lisa wondered at her temerity in speaking her mind the way she had done. Not that she regretted it for an instant. She couldn't have gone on bottling it up very much longer, whatever the consequences.

They had left their things in the charge of one of the lifeguards. Regaining them, they moved by unspoken consent to a spot out of earshot of any other group. Seated with arms supported across bent knees, Reece allowed his gaze to rove her face for a long moment before saying anything.

'You sure about this?' he asked at length.

'Totally,' she said. She gave a small, nervous laugh. 'It wasn't exactly love at first sight, but I think the antagonism was probably a part of it. The only reason I disliked Sandra so much was because she appeared to be with you.'

One dark eyebrow lifted quizzically. 'The *only* reason?'

Her laugh came again, more confidently this time. 'Well, perhaps not. She isn't really my kind of person.'

'Mine either.' He made a wry gesture. 'An error of judgement on my part ever getting involved with her. If it's of any interest, the commitment was all on her side. I'm not sure what she imagined she was going to achieve by booking herself on the tour, but it wouldn't have worked even if you hadn't happened on the scene.'

'She was crazy about you—the way I am.' Not looking at him, she tagged on swiftly, 'You don't have to say anything. I realise I'm jumping the gun. It just isn't in me to hold back on something as important to me as this.'

It was a moment or two before he answered. When he did speak it was on a level note. 'What about Price?'

Her head came up and round with a jerk, her expression nonplussed. 'Dean? What about him?'

The grey eyes were penetrating. 'There's nothing between you?'

'Of course not!' She could hardly believe he was serious. 'Why on earth should you think that?'

His shrug was brief. 'Just that I keep seeing things that might suggest it. Like this morning, for instance—the way you were watching him with those two girls at the market stop. Then, how he put his hand on you when he came to fetch you back to the bus. That was no casual touch just to draw attention.'

'It's just the way he is,' she said. 'Providing they're under forty and reasonably attractive, all females get the same treatment.'

Reece hadn't shifted his gaze from her face. 'He never made any approach to you?'

'No.' The denial was instinctive, and once out impossible to retract. 'I'm not his type.'

'According to what you were saying a moment ago, you fit the criterion.'

'But he doesn't fit mine.' Lisa made an effort to treat the subject with suitable lack of intensity. 'He's a lightweight, Reece.'

'True.' The hard features relaxed a little. 'There aren't many women capable of that much discernment.' He reached out and ran a hand round the back of her neck, caressing the sensitive spot at her nape. 'I should warn you, I'm possessive. If we're going to make it together you'll need to bear it in mind.'

His touch was swimming her senses, but her natural instincts were not subdued. 'If we're going to make it at all, it would need to be a joint understanding. I'm not into sharing either.'

'Point taken and agreed on.' He was smiling now. 'One woman is enough when she's the right one.' There was a pause, a change of tone. 'I never used the word love before. Not in any serious context.'

A warm happiness was spreading through her. She smiled back at him tremulously. 'I'm glad.'

Grey eyes kindled. 'We should have stayed back at the motel. I can't do what I'd like to do to you here.'

'We could always,' she suggested softly, 'go back. The car doesn't have to be turned in right away, does it?'

'I booked it out until Saturday morning,' he said. 'Tomorrow we'll drive down to San Diego. I'd like you to meet my grandmother. She's eighty-three, and a real character.'

'I can't.' Lisa knew real regret. 'I'm taking the Universal tour.'

'Just the one busload, isn't it? Price can do it.'

'I promised to keep an eye on Ben Fuller. I couldn't rely on Dean to do that.' She paused, viewing his expression with rueful eyes. 'It's my job, Reece. I can't just walk away from it.'

'Considering it's in my own interests, I don't expect it.' The shrug was philosophical. 'We can always fly down later and see her. She isn't going to run away.'

Lisa said hesitantly, 'I don't suppose you'll be joining us tomorrow?'

'Too right. Not my kind of entertainment.' He reached for his shirt. 'We can dry off as we go.'

Lisa made no protest. A damp ride was a small price to pay for the pleasure to come. To be in Reece's arms with the knowledge that he felt the same way she did was all she wanted right now. Everything else could go by the board.

They took the same route back for the simple reason that it was the quickest. Head back against the rest, the wind rippling through her hair, Lisa thought she had never felt happier in her life. Everything was working out. Not just a future here in America, but one in which Reece would be playing a major part. He hadn't actually asked her to marry him yet, but he would. His whole attitude was geared towards it. She wasn't looking beyond that event.

They were back at the motel by four-thirty. Making love in the afternoon was somehow enhanced by the very fact that it was full daylight outside, Lisa acknowledged as Reece drew the blind against any intrusive glance from those using the shared balcony approach to their rooms. There were people in the pool almost immediately below; she could hear distant voices and occasional laughter. She wanted to laugh out loud with sheer elation herself.

The sand they had been unable to brush away from damp skin had dried into gritty particles impossible to get rid of entirely. It was Reece who suggested they took a shower together, Reece who turned on the water and drew her into the bath-length cubicle along with him.

The force of the jet took her breath. He turned it down a little and reached for the soap, working up a lather over her shoulders and breasts with slow, smooth movements that made her tremble both inside and out, travelling down gradually over waist and hips to linger for interminable, soul-shaking moments on the twin hemispheres of her buttocks before sliding down to encircle the tops of her thighs. His thumbs brushed the sensitive inner flesh in a caress that sent wave after wave of tremoring sensation through her entire body, making her gasp and dig her fingers into the unyielding muscles of his arms—making her writhe in mindless pleasure as he continued the delicate stimulation. No amount of water could put out the fire he was stoking inside her. She was consumed by it, every inch of her alight with desire. The shuddering sigh was torn from the very depths of her being.

Seizing the second bar of soap, she commenced to follow his lead, not looking at his face at all but concentrating all her attention on the fine hard body beneath her fingers. His shoulders were so broad and strong; she traced each and every muscle, creating whorls of white foam over the taut and glistening skin. She felt the heavy thudding of his heart as she moved down over his chest, the tensing of muscle and sinew beneath the wiry curl of his body hair.

His waist was firm and narrow, with no outward curve over iron-clad hipbone, his thighs inflexible. She heard the breath hiss through his teeth as her hand closed about him, felt the answering ripple of sheer exultation of knowing what she could do to him. Possession was a two-way affair—an experience to be shared, not taken. With Reece she could share anything and everything.

They dried each other with a measured thoroughness, both of them aware of a measured building of tension. Tossing both towels aside, Reece bent and slid an arm beneath her knees, lifting her to chest-height to plant a burning kiss on her eager mouth. He carried her with ease out to the bed and laid her down on top of the cover.

Lisa wound her fingers into the thick dark hair as he dropped his head to her breast. His mouth was a torment; she could barely stand the flickering agony of his tongue on tender, swollen flesh. She could hear a voice saying his name, the sound so guttural she hardly realised it was coming from her own throat.

'I love you,' she whispered huskily. 'Oh, God, Reece, I love you!'

He choked off the words by covering her mouth with his own, the tongue that had coaxed her nipples into the tautly aching peaks of desire now probing the inner softness with demanding passion. And she was answering in kind, straining to be closer, to merge wholly with this man she could never, ever have enough of. Her limbs opened to him, hands reaching, guiding, sliding up to dig frantic fingers into the broad back as he thrust to the very centre of her being, body moving to his rhythm, faster, faster, faster, until the room itself was spinning and nothing else existed but the flooding, mind-stripping ecstasy of being one with Reece.

'I think,' he said gruffly, some time later, 'I'll need to keep myself pretty fit to deal with you. Whoever it was that suggested all Englishwomen were frigid didn't know what they were talking about!'

'Probably a man incapable of rousing one for himself,' murmured Lisa against his chest. 'It's called sour grapes.' She stirred reluctantly. 'The sun's gone over the building. It must be late.'

'And we're supposed to be going to the Bowl.' He gave a sudden chuckle. 'Sounds vaguely familiar.'

Cinderella, thought Lisa mistily, had nothing on her! Fairy stories didn't only happen in books.

'What do I wear?' she asked, and heard the laugh come again.

'That's one characteristic all women share! Whatever you like, honey.' He kissed her hair, and put her gently aside to sit up and reach for his clothing, grimacing as he pulled on the black trunks. 'Talk about a hair shirt!'

Lisa lay and watched him dress. She felt so deliciously lethargic—like a cat satiated with cream. He might be leaving her for now, but she would be seeing him again in a little while. She could live till then—just.

'Half an hour, no more,' he said before departing. 'We'll eat after the show.'

She forced herself into action as the door closed in his wake. Half an hour wasn't long in which to repair the ravages she was sure he had wrought. Crossing the room, she caught sight of herself in the mirror, pausing to view her reflection with a sense of surprise that she could look so normal after the events of the past couple of hours. Apart from a certain puffiness about her lips, and one or two reddened marks here and there, there was little physical sign of that passionate encounter. Only when had her eyes ever glowed that way before? Emerald-bright, they were the true mirrors.

No other man could ever mean as much to her as Reece did, she thought with fervour. He fulfilled every need.

CHAPTER ELEVEN

HOLLYWOOD BOWL by night was a wonderland of light and sound set beneath a canopy of stars. Listening to the music soaring up and out from the wide white dome, feeling Reece's presence at her side, Lisa was in a seventh heaven.

It was almost too much, she found herself thinking at one point. She had to come down to earth and start considering the future. That Reece intended there to be one for them both was evident, but the detail still had to be worked out. No way could she contemplate the kind of lifestyle his mother led. She was too accustomed to working for a living to simply sit back and accept a role as wife and mother.

That latter thought brought a sudden deep-down glow, surfacing in a blush as Reece turned a quizzical glance her way.

'Grieg not to your taste?' he asked softly. 'We could always leave.'

She shook her head in vigorous protest, and settled her mind to the here and now. There was all the time in the world for the rest.

They waited for the main crush to disperse after the concert ended, emerging eventually on to a concourse still busy but at least no longer thronged to capacity. Someone called Reece's name. Turning with him, Lisa's initial attention was centred on the blonde-haired woman in white whose facial features reminded her at once of

Sandra. It was only vaguely that she took in the man at her back.

'It's been an age since we saw you!' exclaimed the newcomer. 'How are you?'

'Making out.' Reece's tone was easy. 'Nice to see you, Charlene. You too, Max,' addressing the balding man in the conservative dark suit who had now drawn level. Reece slid an arm across Lisa's shoulders. 'Meet the Bartons. Lisa Cunningham, from England.'

Charlene's smile lacked any hint of her counterpart's condescension. 'Well, hi! This your first trip Stateside?'

Lisa found herself smiling back involuntarily. 'Yes, it is.'

'So what do you think of us?' Blue eyes went to the arm still about Lisa's shoulders, and she laughed. 'I guess that's a loaded question!'

'I like the country, I like the people,' Lisa returned without a flicker, and drew another laugh, this time from Max Barton himself.

'A nation of diplomats, that's the English!'

'In which case I won't mention July the fourth to come,' she said blandly.

Max slanted an appreciative smile. 'Wit *and* beauty. You always did have a good eye, Reece.'

Just for a moment there was some faint tension in the air. Charlene was the one to break it up. 'We're going on to Scandia's for supper. How about making it a foursome?'

'Why not?' said Reece. 'We'll see you down there.'

They parted at the car park to find their respective vehicles. Lisa waited until they were out of the Bowl gates and heading back to Sunset before making any comment.

'I gather you've known the Bartons a long time?'

'Max and I were in college together,' Reece confirmed.

'And Charlene?'

'She was there too.' He cast a sideways glance. 'Is there a point to this?'

'Not really.' Lisa kept her tone light. 'Just curiosity.'

'It killed the cat.' He pulled to a halt at the lights, added evenly, 'If you caught any hint of innuendo back there you're reading it wrong.'

'Meaning there was never anything between you and Charlene?'

His laugh was short. 'If you want it in black and white, she was my girl before she was his. Max likes to remind me of it, that's all.'

'He took her away from you?'

'It happens.' His foot went down as the lights changed to green. 'If you're after a résumé of my love-life to date, you're going to be out of luck. I'm not asking you about your past.'

'I don't have one.'

There was tolerance in his smile. 'So we'll have to make the future worthwhile.'

She rested her cheek for a brief moment against his shoulder, unable to control the surge of emotion. He was right. Nothing that had happened before they met was of importance.

The restaurant lobby and bar were awash with people. Overbooking, Lisa learned from Charlene, was a regular occurrence. Whether Max had any special pull or had simply slipped the *maître d'* a hefty tip wasn't certain. Whichever, they were shown to a table within ten minutes of arrival.

So far as food went, Lisa had never eaten better. She began with the Viking Platter, which consisted of tiny blinis flavoured with aquavit and topped with caviare and sour cream, followed by a *filet mignon* that melted in the mouth. She laughingly shook her head to the dessert trolley and settled for coffee.

'Many suppers like this one and I'd be like a barrel!' she exclaimed with rueful inflection. 'I'll never sleep tonight!'

Catching Reece's eye, she felt her colour come up, and hoped the others hadn't noticed. Not that she had anything to be ashamed of. Theirs was no casual relationship. All the same, it would be nice if he made that fact a little more obvious to these friends of his.

In the event, it was left to Charlene herself to voice the question when the two of them retired to the ladies' cloakroom to effect repairs before leaving.

'You and Reece serious?' she asked on a casual note as she powdered her nose at the mirror.

Lisa took care with her answer. 'We haven't known each other all that long, but I think so.'

'Considering he's planning on sticking with the tour all the way through, you could be right. He never was the conventional type.' The last with a certain wistfulness. 'There was a time way back when we had something going for us, only he wasn't ready to settle down. He and Max shared a room at college. We just seemed to drift together in the end.' Her tone altered a fraction. 'You realise he's no holy Joe?'

Lisa forced a shrug, a light rejoinder. 'I'd hardly expect any man his age to have been a monk.'

'Oh, I'm not just talking about his personal affairs. He can be pretty ruthless all along the line when it takes him. He didn't get where he is by right of birth. His father was self-made, and believes in everybody starting from the bottom. They're alike in a lot of respects. You didn't meet him yet?'

Lisa shook her head. 'Only his mother.'

'How did you get along with her?'

'I'm not sure,' Lisa confessed. 'She doesn't give much away.'

'That's Elise. She was an actress before she married Reece's father. Quite a good one, by all accounts. Took to the high life like a duck to water. She's one of the city's society queens.' There was a pause, another slight change of tone. 'The Frisco scene can be pretty daunting for an outsider.'

'I expect it can.' Not for anything, Lisa thought, was she going to reveal her inner feelings. 'Shall we go back to the men? They're going to be wondering what's keeping us so long.'

She was relieved when Reece declined Charlene's suggestion that they adjourn to a nightclub to finish off the evening. Max, too, seemed ready to call it a day. They took their leave amicably enough, although Lisa was conscious of Charlene's disappointment. That she still harboured some depth of feeling for Reece was apparent. She wondered if Max knew it too.

It was a straight run back to the motel. Parking the car, Reece said steadily, 'So what did Charlene tell you?'

There was no point beating about the bush, Lisa decided. He had her too well taped. 'She said you were a ruthless character,' she responded lightly. 'Are you, Reece?'

'Depends how you look at it.' He had switched off the engine and was half turned towards her, an elbow resting on the wheel. His eyes were in shadow. 'I don't let anyone get the better of me if I can help it. That isn't to say it never happened. I'm in no way invulnerable.'

'I'm glad,' she said. 'I'm not sure I could live up to the other.'

'How about with?'

She made herself hold the dark gaze. 'Is that a proposition or a proposal?'

His laugh held genuine amusement allied to something both warmer and deeper. 'Which would you prefer it to be?'

'Don't play games with me,' she begged. 'You know how I feel about you, Reece.'

'I guess I'm beginning to.' He ran a finger gently down her cheek, following the line of her jaw to the corner of her mouth. 'Marriage is a big step. I've seen too many go wrong to take it lightly. Love's only a part of it. There has to be compatibility too.'

Lisa swallowed on the sudden hard lump in her throat. 'You don't think we have enough in common?'

'I think maybe we should wait until we're back in Frisco and able to take a clearer view,' he said. 'We've been thrown together in odd circumstances. You might not feel the same way you do now.'

He was giving them both a get-out, she thought achingly. He still wasn't sure enough to commit himself wholesale. 'It's probably a good idea,' she agreed, and wondered at her ability to dissemble when the world she had built up was threatening to fall apart after all. 'Not for me, but for you.'

'Oh, to hell with it!' Voice thickened, he slid his hand around behind her neck and drew her towards him. 'It's marriage or nothing,' he said against her lips. 'We'll learn as we go.'

Dean's announcement at lunch the following day that he would be joining the Universal tour came as a total surprise. Had it not been for her promise to Ben, he could have taken over the whole thing, Lisa reflected wryly.

Not that it really mattered now as Reece had left earlier on some unstated mission. She wouldn't be seeing him again until this evening. Dean or no Dean, she had the afternoon to get through.

'Something wrong?' asked the latter with bland intonation, watching her face. 'Maybe I should have let you know this morning before Harland took off.'

'It wouldn't have made any difference,' she said. 'I promised Ben's mother I'd keep an eye on him.'

'I told her we'd both keep an eye on the two of them.' Blue eyes registered her reaction with a flicker of amusement. 'June not tell you she was coming too? No big deal. There's room enough.'

'I thought you were steering clear of her?' Lisa demanded. 'She's just a kid, Dean!'

'But devoted, and I'm in the mood for a bit of hero worship.' He was totally unrepentant. 'You'll be there right along with us. You *and* young Benjamin. Always supposing we don't get separated, that is.'

She would make sure of it, Lisa told herself emphatically. It would at least keep her mind occupied with matters other than those filling it at present. Marriage with Reece was no longer a source of conjecture. He had made that clear enough last night. The when was still to be decided, of course, but there was no tearing hurry. It was enough to know it would happen at some point.

There were other things to sort out too. Such as her role in life. There was no reason why she shouldn't still take on that PA job he had spoken of. Plenty of husbands and wives worked well together. Or if he didn't care for that idea, there had to be other positions available within the company. Given the opportunity, she could prove herself no deadweight.

Judging from the look on Ben's face when the party assembled in the car park, he hadn't known his sister was to be joining them either. Mrs Fuller came to wave them off. What she and her husband had planned for the afternoon, Lisa didn't know, but she doubted if the woman would enjoy her few hours of freedom from family commitment.

They took the Hollywood Freeway out to Universal City and the huge studio lot and theme park opened up to public entertainment. The tour itself was conducted on company trams, with each party of approximately one hundred and twenty being allocated a separate departure time. While waiting, there was no shortage of things to do and see. Ben was eager to visit the *Miami Vice* set where stand-in actors played out an action-packed episode with realistic special effects. After that it was on to the stuntmen and another fifteen minutes of mayhem.

Dean and June disappeared during the latter show. One minute they were there, the next gone. Lisa contemplated going to look for the pair of them, but with so many thousands of people milling around it would be a fairly hopeless task. Ben accepted the situation without concern. Dean, he said, was more than welcome to his sister's company.

There was still no sign of the pair when their turn came to take the studio tour. Lisa sat through an hour and a half of flash floods, collapsing bridges, shark attacks and a simulated earthquake scheduled to give the strongest nerve a jolt. Ben was entranced by it all, and would willingly have gone round again had it been allowed.

'The best ever!' he exclaimed when they finally returned to the starting point. He gave Lisa a wide, bright smile. 'Thanks. If it hadn't been for you I'd have missed it. Now I'll really have something to tell the kids at school about!'

'Not the rest?' she asked.

He shook his head. 'I didn't want to come on this holiday, although it would have been OK if we'd gone to Florida like Mum first said. I'm fed up of sitting about on a coach.'

'If you want to be a courier, there'll be quite a lot of that to do,' Lisa warned.

'Depends what kind. Some are based at hotels, aren't they?' He shrugged thin shoulders. 'Anyway, it's going to be another four years before I get out of school.'

Lisa smiled sympathetically. 'It will pass. Get a few good A Levels under your belt, and you'll be able to pick and choose.'

From the look on his face, it wasn't the first time he had heard that piece of advice. He slanted a glance, and said unexpectedly, 'Are you going to marry that American?'

'What makes you think I might?' she queried on a cautious note.

'Dad said you were getting it together.'

Cheeks burning, she made an effort to retain her sense of humour. 'Just between you and me, the answer is yes. I'd rather it wasn't spread around.'

'I shan't tell anybody.' He added with emphasis, 'I'm never going to get married. It's like putting your head in a noose!'

Another of his father's ill-considered remarks, no doubt, Lisa thought drily. She made no reply. Ben would eventually reach an age where he could start running his own life. Until then, he had to weather through.

Dean and June turned up two minutes before the coach was due to leave, much to her relief. The latter looked thoroughly self-satisfied.

'We've had a super afternoon!' she said without going into detail. 'We weren't bothered about the silly tour.'

Dean left her to join her brother at the rear of the coach, and came to sit beside Lisa at the front.

'If you're going to start reading me the riot act,' he said smoothly, 'you've got half an hour.'

'I wouldn't waste my breath,' she retorted. 'You realise her parents are going to hear it all from Ben, of course?'

He laughed. 'June can take care of little brother OK. She's no slouch when it comes to getting what she wants.'

'And did she?' The question was jerked from her.

The blue eyes sparked maliciously. 'That would be telling. You've no room to talk, anyway. Think I don't know how you've been spending your nights lately?'

Lisa bit her lip. It might only be a guess on his part, but he had a point. 'June's sixteen,' she said. 'You can find plenty of girls nearer your own age without bothering with schoolgirls.'

'Except that the one girl on this trip nearer my own age found a bigger fish.'

'Don't lay the blame at my door,' she shot back at him. 'If you were the only man on earth I'd still have no interest! Either stay away from June from now on, or I'll report the whole thing to head office!'

'Fire away. I already fixed up that job here in LA. It'll just be a case of picking up my things in Frisco and heading right back.' His face had tautened. 'You'll get yours one of these days!'

There was just no point, Lisa decided, in continuing this conversation—if it could be called that. She had handled things badly from the beginning; it was too late now to start over.

They finished the journey back downtown in silence. Dean made no move to get up when they pulled in at the motel. Lisa had to press past his knees in order to reach the doors.

She stood as usual at the top of the steps until everyone had alighted, receiving the various comments with a smile and a suitable reply. June hesitated at Dean's side, but he made no response and she was left with no recourse but to follow her brother from the vehicle. Lisa's heart went out to the girl. She knew only too well how she must be feeling. Hopefully, there would be no repercussions.

Dean waited until everyone was off before getting to his feet. Dropping down the two steps ahead of him, Lisa was stunned to feel his arms snake around her waist as they reached the ground, holding her tightly while he planted a brief kiss on the temple turned back towards him.

'Just a token gesture,' he said in her ear, and released her again.

Halfway up the outside staircase to the second storey, June glowered down at them. Following her fierce flight up and along the balcony, Lisa saw Reece leaning on the rail outside his room door, and knew at once what Dean's game was. The latter was already moving away, the smile on his face all the confirmation needed. Try explaining that away, it said.

Reece gave her a calculated regard as she approached along the walkway. 'Had a good time?' he asked.

'So-so.' There was only one way to handle the situation and that was head on, she decided. 'The bit of by-play you just saw was purely for your benefit,' she said. 'Dean's way of paying me back.'

Reece lifted an eyebrow. 'For what?'

'Hauling him over the coals for playing around with June Fuller.'

'I thought he wasn't supposed to be going on the Universal trip?' he said.

'He wasn't. It was a last-minute decision on his part.' She made a small, appealing gesture. 'Reece, there's nothing between us. I swear it! You don't really believe I'd jeopardise everything for someone like *him*, do you?'

The shrug was brief, his face reflecting little change of expression. 'It's been known.'

Her temper flared suddenly and fiercely. Not for anything was she going to beg! 'So forget it!' she said thickly. 'Just forget the whole thing!'

He came after her as she swung back towards her own room, taking the key from her fingers to insert it in the lock and push open the door. Lisa turned to face him as he followed her in.

'If you've any doubts about me, I'd as soon you didn't bother,' she flung at him. 'I can manage without you!'

He reached out and yanked her towards him, holding her head still between both hands while he kissed her with almost savage intent. 'What the hell was I supposed to think?' he demanded roughly when she stopped struggling against him. 'He's a good-looking guy.'

'So are you,' she protested, and saw his mouth take on a sardonic slant.

'I'm not in need of a morale-booster. All I'm saying is it looked pretty convincing from where I was standing.'

'So maybe I should have slapped his face.' Her jaw hurt from the pressure of his cupped hands. She added with control, 'If you don't let me go I'm going to finish up with a stiff neck.'

'Better that than a broken one.' He studied her for a moment, eyes piercing, then he sighed and released his grip. 'No man likes to think he's being made a fool of. I'm no exception.'

'I'm not trying to make a fool of you,' she said. 'I love you, Reece. Haven't I proved it?'

'By going to bed with me?' His smile was faint. 'That's hardly conclusive.'

'It is where I'm concerned.' Her voice tremored. 'I don't make a habit of it. Can you say the same?'

This time the smile was accompanied by a shrug. 'With more validity than many, maybe. We're not talking about previous affairs. They're not important. This is.'

'To me too. More than anything else could ever be.' Lisa laid her cheek against the broad hard chest, feeling the steady beat of his heart. 'How could there be anything between Dean and me? You and I have spent almost every spare moment together this last week.'

'True enough.' Reece put a hand on the back of her neck, turning her face up to his. His eyes had lost the steely look. 'I warned you I was the possessive type. Until I met you, I hadn't realised just how much so. I'm not likely to turn into one of those husbands who can't even stand to see their wives so much as talking to another man, but there's a limit.' He dropped his head to find her mouth again, this time with a gentler intent. 'You'd better think about getting changed,' he added with reluctance. 'We're driving down to Long Island for dinner. A little seafood place I know.'

Lisa didn't care where they were going. They were back on level footing again, and that was all that mattered. Dean's little ruse hadn't worked.

CHAPTER TWELVE

FROM Los Angeles to Monterey was the longest day's drive of the whole tour: more than three hundred miles through coastal towns and fishing villages, and the dramatic twists and turns of Big Sur.

They lunched at San Luis Obispo in a bright pink inn that was pure kitsch both inside and out. Reece made notes for a change of venue here. There were plenty of more conducive places at which to eat, he said. No point in striking a sour note where it wasn't necessary, especially towards the end of the tour when people were already beginning to come down off the vacational high.

'It's back to the grind come Monday morning for all of us,' he added lightly. 'Another day, another dollar!'

'Not for me,' Lisa reminded him. 'My job ends when we reach San Francisco.' She paused, not quite sure how to approach the subject. 'Does the offer you made still stand?'

Reece gave her a quizzical look. 'Which one?'

She laughed. 'The first. You said I'd made a good PA, remember?'

It was difficult to tell from his expression what he might be thinking. 'You're expecting to work?'

'Well, I certainly don't intend sitting around twiddling my thumbs,' she said. 'Marriage isn't a full-time job.'

His mouth tilted. 'So long as I can lay claim to the night shift. We'll talk about it later. Time we were back on the road if we want to make Monterey in time for some sightseeing.'

With which she would have to be content for the time being, she acknowledged. At least he wasn't coming the chauvinist and refusing to contemplate a working wife.

Studying the angles and planes of his face as he counted out notes to cover the bill, she felt that familiar melting sensation inside. He was so much the dominant male, yet capable of bending to her will too. That combination was rare indeed. To lose him now would be devastating. Only she wasn't going to lose him, was she? The emotion wasn't one-sided. Reece loved her the way she loved him, and it was out of this world!

Carmel and Monterey were almost side by side. Backed by low hills thick with cypresses, the former was a haven of tree-lined streets and alleys housing art galleries and quaint little craft shops. Reminiscent of some small English towns, Lisa thought with a pang of homesickness swiftly blanked out. This was her home now. If she went back at all it would only be to visit. There was nothing to draw her back.

'Pity we didn't get to see Clint,' moaned one of the woman passengers regretfully. 'I've seen every movie he ever made!'

'More than once,' remarked her husband with wry inflection. 'I never get to use the video!'

Monterey had its own Fisherman's Wharf like a smaller version of Pier Thirty-Nine back in San Francisco, while Steinbeck's Cannery Row a couple of miles away had been converted to much the same touristy collection of trendy restaurants and shopping complexes.

'The price of progress,' agreed Reece when Lisa mourned the loss of atmosphere. 'We'll go downtown

for dinner. Somewhere special, seeing it's the last night
of the tour.'

With tomorrow the first day of the rest of her life,
thought Lisa, shrugging inwardly at the banality of the
phrase. Who cared? It was fitting. She was closing one
door and opening another.

They were booked into a motel out at the Monterey
Fairgrounds. Showered and ready but for the dress she
had selected to wear for the evening, she was about to
slide into it when the knock came on the door. Smiling
at her instinctive reaction, she left the dress where it was
on the bed and went to answer it. Reece had seen her in
far less than the flimsy black briefs and brassiere, and
would be doing so again later. In the meantime, there
was no harm in a little tantalisation.

The sight of Dean standing outside was too much of
a surprise for any immediate response. He didn't wait
for any, shouldering his way into the room in a manner
that jerked her out of the momentary suspension and
into flaring anger.

'What do you think you're doing?' she demanded.
'Get out of here!'

'Not until I've got what I'm after,' he said without
turning a hair. He closed the door again, blue eyes
glinting with malice as he surveyed her slender curves.
'Nice! Can't say I blame Harland for staying with it so
long.'

Lisa had backed involuntarily away from him, but she
refused to shrink under the sneering gaze. 'Whatever it
is you have in mind,' she said, 'you can't possibly
imagine I'm just going to go along with it? If you're not
out of here in one minute I'm going to call Reception
and have you put out!'

He lounged against the near wall, making no attempt to come any closer. 'Not lover-boy? Why? Scared he might misconstrue?' His smile was slow. 'Guess he might at that. Most men would—especially after the other incidents I set up for him.'

She stared at him, only now beginning to realise just how deep the enmity went. Dean had planned this down to the last detail—right from Page when he had discovered Reece's true identity, if she wasn't mistaken. Allied to her refusal to respond to his overtures, that failure to pass on the information must have been the last straw. Given the opportunity, he could act any present-day movie star right off the screen, came the fleeting thought.

'This is ridiculous,' she said. 'All right, so I could have been a little more considerate this last week or two, but that's no cause to go this far, surely?'

There was no lessening of intent in the icy blue gaze. 'Every cause,' he returned. 'I don't have to take what you dished out lying down. You think you've got it made with Harland, don't you? I aim to prove you wrong.'

As if on cue, footsteps sounded outside on the landing, and a shadow passed the curtained window. Lisa stiffened at the knock on the door. There was nothing she could do to stop the next few minutes from happening. All she could hope was that Reece would be prepared to listen to her. Only from what he had said earlier, it was doubtful. Dean had set her up so carefully. Looking back now over the last few days, she could think of a dozen occasions when his actions might have been misconstrued.

He put up a hand and ruffled his hair before moving to answer the summons. About to repeat the knock, Reece stood with fist suspended, the smile wiped from his face as his gaze shifted from Dean to the scantily clad figure beyond.

'Just leaving,' said the younger man. 'She's all yours now, so——'

He got no further for the simple reason that his throat was constricted by the hand seizing hold of his shirt front. Jaw muscles clenched, eyes narrowed to blazing slits, Reece jerked him out through the doorway and up against the jamb, the fist he hadn't yet unfolded drawing back with obvious intent.

'Don't!' The cry was torn from Lisa's lips. 'He isn't worth it!'

For a brief moment it was touch and go, then slowly he lowered his fist and released the man whose face had lost a great deal of its normal colour.

'You've got ten minutes to clear the place,' he clipped. 'You'll be paid what's owing but you're through as of now. Clear?'

Dean straightened his shirt front with a hand not quite steady. 'You can't do that. I'm entitled to finish off this trip at least.'

'So sue.' Reece left him standing there, coming into the room and closing the door with a deliberation that made Lisa's blood run cold. 'You damned little tramp!' he gritted.

'It isn't true,' she said desperately. 'He was just trying to ruin things for us, that's all.'

'Why?' he demanded. 'Why would he go to all that trouble?'

'Because I didn't tell him about you, for one thing—and because I turned him down.'

His lips curled. 'Hardly good enough reason.'

'Not for you, perhaps, but Dean's kind don't take kindly to rejection.' She made a small gesture of appeal.

'I was probably at fault for being too blunt. There are ways and ways. I chose the wrong one.'

'Clever,' he said, 'but not convincing. I've suspected something going on between you two from the start, but I let myself be duped. Only not any more. I'll be flying back to Frisco tonight. Tomorrow you turn in your gear and then get the hell out. Your two weeks' salary will be forwarded—along with a bonus for extra-curricular services rendered. It's been——' he paused, the skin about his mouth whitening under the pressure '—quite an experience.'

Her cheeks burned. Any further appeal was obviously going to be useless. She had nothing to lose by having her say. Eyes dark, she gave it to him from the shoulder.

'I was wrong about you too, Reece. I thought you were different. Turns out there's little to choose between you and Dean, when it comes right down to it. You're both of you so concerned with salvaging your precious male egos, you can't even see straight!' Her laugh was bitter. 'And I thought I loved you. Just goes to show what fools women are!'

The grey eyes blazed with a sudden dangerous light. He reached her in a couple of swift strides, pulling her up against him to find her mouth in a kiss that seared. The fingers at her back were too practised in the art to be foiled by her wildly groping, protesting hand. Freed of their flimsy covering, her breasts sprang into quivering expectancy, her whole body trembling beneath the crude onslaught.

'Act like a tramp and you'll get treated like a tramp,' he gritted between clenched teeth. 'I'll show you the difference!'

She tore herself away from him with the strength born of fury, too incensed by the hurtfulness and unfairness of his accusation to stand there and take whatever else he cared to dish out.

'If you don't go I'll start screaming,' she threatened. 'I mean it, Reece!'

For a moment she thought he was going to ignore the warning. He made a move towards her, then stopped abruptly, shaking his head in grim negation. 'That's one trick you're not going to get the chance to pull on me. If you want to catch up with Price, you'd better be quick about it. I dare say the drivers can handle what's left of the tour.'

'I'm seeing it through,' she declared. 'Whether you believe it or not, I don't have any interest in what Dean does from here.'

'A pity you didn't cut loose earlier, then. I might never have known for sure.' He gave her a final contemptuous scrutiny before turning away. 'Your choice.'

Her loss, she thought numbly as the door closed in his wake. The love of her life had turned out to be nothing but an illusion.

Saying goodbye to everyone on the Sunday afternoon proved a trial. The British contingent were to transfer straight to the airport for the evening flight to Heathrow. Lisa almost wished she were going with them.

June Fuller had reacted to Dean's disappearance with apathy, unlike the rest of the passengers who had wanted to know the whys and wherefores. Lisa had managed to come up with some plausible tale of family illness requiring his immediate presence, but had found it far more difficult to explain Reece's absence. In the end, she had settled for business commitments, and left it to each individual to put their own interpretation on that. It didn't matter, anyway. Nothing mattered very much at present.

Ben took his leave on a note of despondency mixed with relief to be going home. The tour had been OK, he said, but he wouldn't want to do another. Lisa shared that particular sentiment. Given a few days to make preparations, she intended heading for pastures new herself. Where exactly, she wasn't yet sure. Anywhere except America. She had had her fill of this country.

Jane had driven in to pick her up at the depot. Answering her questions regarding the trip on the way back to the apartment without giving herself away wasn't easy. It was obvious that the other suspected something amiss, although she waited until they were seated in the small but comfortable living-room with a welcome cup of coffee in front of them before giving voice.

'I gather it wasn't all a bed of roses?' she said. 'What went wrong?'

Lisa smiled and shrugged. 'A few hiccups here and there. Nothing too drastic. How about you? Anything new to report?'

'Apart from the company being taken over, not a lot.' She said it casually, waiting for the reaction Lisa had to try to conjure convincingly. 'Came as a complete surprise to everybody—including Mr Bucknell, I'd say, from the way he's been acting since the news got out. Apart from that, nothing seems to have changed.'

'No reason why it should, I suppose,' said Lisa. 'It isn't as if the company were losing money. All it means if you're now part of a group.'

'Brecket-Copeland. One of the biggest international conglomerates there is.' It was Jane's turn to shrug. 'I don't suppose there is anything to worry about. If there was going to be any staff pruning at all, we'd have probably heard by now.'

'I'm sure of it.' Lisa finished her coffee and got to her feet. 'I'm going to have a shower and get changed. The uniform will need to be returned.'

'You don't think there's going to be any chance of a permanent job, then?' said Jane.

'None.' Lisa could say that with total certainty. She summoned a lighter note. 'Not to worry. It was a long shot at best.'

'You're more than welcome to stay on here until your visa expires,' Jane offered. 'Something might turn up.'

'Thanks.' There would be time enough, Lisa reflected, to announce her intention of moving on. Jane would be sorry to see her go, but she would get over it. She had made a life for herself here.

Monday morning brought no lessening of depression. It was going to be some time yet before she could begin picking up the threads with a will, Lisa acknowledged. She spent the day pottering about the apartment, and prepared supper for Jane's anticipated arrival at six.

Tomorrow, she would have to get round to making some firm decisions, but for tonight she was going to forget about it, she told herself firmly when she heard the key in the door. She had opened a bottle of wine to go with the spaghetti bolognese. Getting thoroughly tipsy seemed a good idea.

It took only one glance at Jane's face to know that something had gone seriously wrong.

'What happened?' she asked in swift concern, and was halfway there even before the answer came.

'I lost my job,' Jane said wryly. 'I'm out at the end of the month. Mr Bucknell was very apologetic, but he didn't have any choice. He'd been told he was over-staffed. As the last in, it was only fair I should be first out.'

White-hot anger began boiling up in Lisa's veins. It took a real effort to keep her voice level. 'Are you the only redundancy?'

'I think so. I didn't ask.' Jane made an attempt to shake off despondency. 'Something smells good!'

This had to be Reece's doing, Lisa reflected as the other girl went on through to the kitchenette to see what was cooking. The coincidence was too marked to be just that. It wouldn't have taken him long to discover who had put her name forward as replacement for the sick courier—and even less time, it appeared, to act on the information.

The anger was mingled with shock that the man she had loved could turn out to be so far removed from her image of him. That any man could be so vindictive went beyond belief. Wasn't it enough to persecute her for her supposed misdeeds?

He wasn't going to get away with it, she vowed there and then. No matter what it took, she was going to get Jane reinstated! The place to reach him was at his office. It shouldn't be difficult to find out where that was situated.

If anything, her resolve strengthened overnight. She said nothing to Jane. There was no point in going into detail until she had this thing sorted. The Brecket-Copeland divisional offices were located in Pacific Heights. Bypassing the ground-floor reception desk by waiting for a moment when a whole group of people were claiming attention, Lisa checked the lift directory before embarking for the appropriate floor.

In a few minutes she was going to be seeing Reece again, if she had to storm his office to do so. Anger was her bolster against other infiltrating emotions. Facing him, with the memory of his scorn and contempt still searing her mind and heart, was going to take every ounce of will-power she possessed.

The lift gave directly on to a luxuriously appointed office area. Seated behind a vast curved desk covered in leather and bearing every modern-day aid to efficient business procedure, the well-groomed young woman looked up from her console with an enquiring lift of her pencilled eyebrows at Lisa's approach.

'Can I help you?' she asked.

'I'd like to see Mr Harland,' Lisa supplied.

The smile was perfunctory. 'I'm afraid Mr Harland doesn't see anyone without an appointment.'

There were only two doors leading from the room, Lisa had already noted. She took a chance on the nearest, ignoring the protest as she made purposefully for it. Made of a polished wood not unlike mahogany, with a handle of solid brass, it opened smoothly to her push, revealing a further large and luxurious room well lit by the picture-window with its distant view of the Golden Gate bridge.

One seated on the far side of the big solid desk, the other standing at the window, the two men *in situ* both looked round at the interruption.

'I said no——' began Reece, breaking off abruptly as recognition dawned. His expression underwent a swift, indecipherable change before settling into lines that set Lisa's heart thudding painfully against her ribcage. 'What the devil are you doing here?' he demanded.

The secretary, or whatever, appeared at Lisa's back, voice apologetic. 'I'm sorry, Mr Harland. She just walked straight past me!'

'And I'm staying,' Lisa stated flatly, taking a grip on herself. 'For as long as it takes to have Jane's job secured, anyway. Of all the low-down tricks to pull, that had to be the lowest, Reece! Why take it out on her for what *I'm* supposed to have done?'

Brows drawn together, he nodded to the other woman. 'I'll deal with this, Lois.' He came to his feet as the door closed, tall and lean and achingly familiar in his firm masculine stance. 'I've no idea what you're talking about,' he said shortly. 'Who is Jane?'

'The girl I'm staying with. The same one who proposed me as replacement on the tour. She's been made redundant, as if you didn't know.' Lisa was giving herself no time to lose impetus. 'Either she's reinstated as of now, or I'll issue a statement to the Press regarding the extra-curricular activities of a certain Brecket-Copeland executive!'

'Quite a mouthful,' commented the silver-haired and distinguished-looking man at the window on a note of amused admiration. 'And so beautifully enunciated! Are you going to introduce us, Reece?'

'Lisa Cunningham—my father,' came the curt response. 'I still don't know what you're talking about. If your friend has lost her job it's unfortunate, but hardly my concern.'

Lisa made a dismissive gesture. 'Don't try to make out it was pure coincidence, because it won't wash. You wanted to get back at me for making a fool of you, didn't you, Reece? It didn't matter who else got hurt in the process, providing your precious pride was salved!'

'My precious pride,' he said tautly, 'isn't the issue. Will you get it through your head that I had nothing to do with what you're accusing me of!'

She gazed at him for a lengthy moment, refusing to believe that he might be telling the truth. 'You'd deny there were any redundancies in the take-over?'

'I don't make that kind of policy.'

'You have jurisdiction over those who do. A word in the right ear would have been all that was necessary.'

'It might be a good idea if I left the two of you to sort this out on your own,' said Richard Harland. He gave his son a frankly speculative glance in passing, turning on a smile for Lisa's benefit as he approached. 'I'd say don't let him get away with anything if I thought it was likely that you might. Perhaps we'll meet again at a more conducive moment?'

Lisa returned the smile, albeit a little stiffly. 'I doubt it.' She added levelly, 'I'm sorry to have interrupted your meeting, Mr Harland, but this can't wait. I have to sort things out before I leave the country.'

'Take your time,' he invited. 'I'll have Reece fill me in on the details later.'

Left alone with the younger man, she made no move to further the argument, waiting for Reece himself to take up the challenge again. He was studying her with narrowed eyes, jawline rock-hard. When he did speak it wasn't what she had expected to hear.

'What was that about leaving the country?

Her shrug was brief. 'There's nothing to stay on for. Jane deserves to have her apartment to herself again. Always providing she can afford to keep it, of course. Green card or no green card, jobs aren't all that easy to come by.' She paused, controlling any tendency towards unevenness in her voice. 'So what about it?'

'I'm telling you for the last time,' he said, 'I had no personal involvement in the matter. Neither am I willing to interfere with decisions already put into operation.' He had moved clear of the desk, standing with feet slightly spread and hands thrust into trouser pockets, pulling the material taut across muscular thighs. 'If your

friend would like to put in an application, I'll have
Personnel find her a new position. How will that do?'

Lisa swallowed on the lump in her throat. 'How can
I be sure you'll follow through?'

'Because whatever else I might be, a liar I'm not,' he
came back hardily. 'Where were you thinking of going
from here?'

Made without change of tone, the question took her
aback for a moment. She rallied with an effort. 'Does
it matter?'

'Yes.' He sounded almost savage about it. 'I've spent
the last couple of nights wanting to kill you, Lisa, but
it doesn't alter the way you can make me feel just by
walking through that door a few minutes ago. I thought
I'd found the one girl in the world I could really trust.
Catching you with Price was like being kicked in the
gut!'

'You didn't catch me *with* him,' she said huskily. 'Not
in the sense you mean. It was all circumstantial.'

He studied her for a long, piercing moment, expression
unrelenting. 'Why not admit it and be done? You're not
gaining either of us anything by pretending it never happened. There's such a thing as starting over. Not as good,
maybe, but worth a try.'

For a fleeting moment she was almost tempted to
accept the offer, but only for a moment. Without trust,
they didn't have anything.

'Goodbye, Reece,' she said flatly. 'I shan't be bothering you again.'

He moved so swiftly she hadn't even finished depress-
ing the door-handle before he reached her. Swinging her
round by the shoulder, he pulled her roughly into his
arms. His mouth on hers was fierce, demanding and
gaining a like response. Lisa clung to him in a kind of

desperation, not thinking, only feeling—wanting—needing.

'It wasn't true,' she murmured against his lips. 'Dean set me up. You have to believe me!'

'I do.' He held her away from him, eyes rueful. 'You convinced me the moment you started to walk out. I'm sorry, Lisa. I should have had more faith in my own judgement.'

'It doesn't matter. Not any more.' She could still scarcely believe it was all coming right again. 'The whole thing happened so quickly. We didn't have time to develop any real foundation. If I'd caught you in a similar situation, I'd have taken it exactly the same way.'

'I doubt it.' His voice was soft, the hands coming up to cup her face tenderly. 'You'd have done what I should have done and given the other party something to think about. If I ever lay eyes on friend Price again I'll take him apart!'

'If you ever do see him again it will probably be between the covers of some magazine,' she said. 'He's going to be a male model.'

'Should just about suit him.' Reece slid an arm about her and guided her to one of the big club chairs set in conversational grouping about a coffee-table, sitting down to pull her on to his knees and kiss her again with consuming passion.

'We're going to be married as soon as it can be arranged,' he stated roughly when he came up for air. 'I'm not wasting any more time.' One lean brown finger traced a gentle line from her temple down over her cheek to outline the shape of her lips, making her tremble with sheer unadulterated desire. 'My own English rose!'

'Thorns and all,' she murmured, and saw the smile she had thought she would never see again curve the strong mouth.

'Handled the right way, they're not too lethal.' His expression changed again to one of wry acknowledgment. 'I came close to losing you, and all because I couldn't bring myself to believe what my senses were telling me. By the time I'd got round to coming to look for you, it would have been too late.'

'Would you?' she asked. 'Have come to look for me, I mean.'

'Eventually. Once I'd managed to come to terms with myself. I can't alter the way I'm made. Not to any extent. I need to be the only man in your life.'

'You are,' she said. 'Reece Harland of San Francisco, USA. The only man I'd ever want!'

Next month's Romances

Each month, you can choose from a world of variety in romance with Mills & Boon. These are the new titles to look out for next month.

UNLIKELY CUPID Catherine George

HEART ON FIRE Charlotte Lamb

BLIND PASSION Anne Mather

WITHOUT KNOWING WHY Jessica Steele

A LITTLE MOONLIGHT Betty Neels

NO WAY TO BEGIN Michelle Reid

ANYTHING FOR YOU Rosemary Hammond

MAGIC CARPETS Lucy Keane

PIRATE'S HOSTAGE Eleanor Rees

A FOOLISH DREAM Emma Richmond

ONCE IN A LIFETIME Jacqueline Gilbert

THE RELUCTANT LOVER Miranda Lee

THE IMPERFECT BRIDE Karen van der Zee

FORGOTTEN LOVE Nicola West

TENDER BETRAYAL Grace Green

STARSIGN
A DESIRE TO LOVE Sally Cook

Available from Boots, Martins, John Menzies, W.H. Smith, Woolworths and other paperback stockists.

Also available from Mills and Boon Reader Service, P.O. Box 236, Thornton Road, Croydon, Surrey CR9 3RU.